SILENT WOLF

He was a loner, known as 'Silent' – because he had had his throat partly ripped out by wolves. He had his own private mission and dead men began to pile up around him. Till a naïve girl who was a mighty good rifle shot joined him and cramped his style. She tried to make him see things differently, but finally, saw them his way. Then the body count climbed again, ending in a final bloody showdown in border mud.

0135723223

SILENT WOLF

SILENT WOLF

by

Jake Douglas

Dales Large Print Books
Long Preston, North Yorkshire,
BD23 4ND, England.

British Library Cataloguing in Publication Data.

Douglas, Jake
   Silent wolf.

   A catalogue record of this book is
   available from the British Library

   ISBN   978-1-84262-677-1 pbk

First published in Great Britain 2008 by Robert Hale Limited

Copyright © Jake Douglas 2008

Cover illustration © Gordon Crabb by arrangement with
Alison Eldred

The right of Jake Douglas to be identified as the author of this
work has been asserted by him in accordance with the
Copyright, Designs and Patents Act, 1988

Published in Large Print 2009 by arrangement with
Robert Hale Ltd.

Dales Large Print is an imprint of Library Magna Books Ltd.

Printed and bound in Great Britain by
T.J. (International) Ltd., Cornwall, PL28 8RW

CHAPTER 1

NIGHT OF THE WOLVES

The wolves had taken over the night.

The moon was high above the sawtooths and the lobos came down out of the Dragoons, driven by the Chiricahuas for a ritual protection of their land. The wolves called to the white orb from every crag and peak and ledge, howling at the sky, from every hidden water-hole and lair where even the cubs were stimulated to add their squeals to the din.

It was one of the mysterious 'gatherings' that the Indians respected. They lay quiet in their wikiups and tipis, listening, comforting the restive children, waiting for moonset and the drifting away of the cries of the lobos.

And the exodus of the intruders.

The cattle herd on the plains snorted and bellowed and stomped. Nighthawks swore softly: *Don't tempt the damn dogs!* Sweaty hands felt for gun butts and rifle stocks.

Many a man's shirt felt suddenly damp around the neck. Tempers were abrasive. Meaningless curses joined the banshee wails drifting down from the Dragoons.

'Get that breakaway, goddamnit, Spud! They'll all follow if one breaks! Get the son of a bitch! *Now!*'

There was a commotion on the north side of the herd as two riders cut across to contain the escape attempt, ropes whistling and slapping dust from quivering hides.

The bellowing wakefulness spread, rose to mingle with the ceaseless howling, then:

'God almighty! What's *that?*'

The entire crew, even the cook, was on herd watch and they all detected the sudden change in the moon-wailing on the nearest slopes.

Snarls that conjured up visions of slavering red jaws and white scimitar teeth. Yelps, high-pitched, pain-ridden. The dominant growl of an aggressor, the whine of the submissive, all of it chilling the blood as the snarls escalated in the unmistakable sounds of a primitive fight – to the death.

'Man! I bet hair'n'hide're flyin' thick an' fast up there on that ridge!'

'Thicker'n flies round a roast of beef! Will you *listen* to that racket!'

'Yeah. Some poor animal's bein' torn apart.'

'Well, that has to be you, Doc! Hell, it's one less "poor animal" to rip the teats off a calvin' cow or bring down a shaky-leg foal! C'mon, you beauty! Rip the throat outta the bastard!'

Others joined in and Doc remained silent, staring up at the dark bulk rising against the stars. Behind him, the herd was moving now: eye-whites rolled, horns clashed.

'Watch 'em!' bellowed the trail boss, Tarne Shiels. 'We don't want a goddamn stampede! Quit yappin an' get ridin'. Remember, you ain't been paid yet!'

'Brace that southern side! Judas priest, brace it!'

The night was full of commands and action now, the mournful, blood-chilling wailing from the slopes adding to the feeling of catastrophe that had suddenly descended upon the trail herd.

There was hard riding needed, and plunging horns to avoid. Slow mounts paid the penalty and shrilled in pain as ivory tips raked their sweating hides. More than one man had his lower legs gashed. Coiled ropes swung and boots drove against laid-back ears and dripping nostrils.

9

They were holding them but only just. If only the damn wolves would shut up, half the terror that filled the night would drift away and the herd would eventually realize it and...

Some of the panicked steers were part-way up the slopes now. Shiels hoarsely directed a couple of riders to get above them and drive them back towards the main herd, which was beginning to resemble a massive millwheel of heaving backs, dust rising to smudge the moonlight. *Getting ready to break...*

It had to happen; within seconds of men being ordered on to the slopes the herd surged into stampede. Shiels swore and reined down; he did the only thing he could then: 'Let 'em run!' he bellowed. At least it was flat...

They would lose several days rounding them up but better that than to try and turn them in this howling darkness; he could lose as many men as steers. They would run themselves out in a wild scattering and that would mean...

Something made him glance up.

He was on the slope, slightly higher than the nighthawks he had sent there, and he glimpsed the thrusting broken edge of a ledge some ten feet above him. He could distinctly hear the snarlings and snappings as wolves fought up there. Stones pattered down around him and he felt the rod of fear solidify from his chest to his belly. Hell, if those blood-lusting lobos slipped over the edge while he was directly underneath...!

He involuntarily put a hand to his throat, his mind picturing it being torn out by savage fangs, but he had delayed just a few moments too long.

Dark, writhing shapes catapulted out from the ledge, twisting and convulsing against the stars as they plunged down on top of him. He threw up a protective arm, forgetting all about his six-gun and everything else as he dived out of the saddle. As he did so there was a heavy thump, the gusting of air from lungs. He flung himself wildly aside as kicking legs and raking claws caught his loose clothing, spinning him on to this face.

A heavy weight rolled over him, crushing the breath out of him briefly. *My God! That wolf must weigh as much as a man!* He felt his bowels quake at the thought of coming up against such a monster. Belatedly he fumbled for his Colt. The holster was empty.

So was his heart when he realized it.

He brought up suddenly against a low rock at the foot of the slope, his grey still running, mane flying, tail straight out like a plume in a high wind. The stampede was going away from him – and so were his men, following his orders.

And then he realized he was not entirely alone on this slope. Dust was settling, gravel was still sliding. There was a dying whimpering only a few feet from where he lay and a deep-throated growl that froze him.

Then a kind of silence. He was aware of the diminishing thunder of the herd, the cries of the riders, and the fading howls of the lobos above. Groping for something to grip so he could heave to his feet, he snatched his hand back as he touched stiff coarse fur – sticky with what had to be blood. He slipped and fell forward, sprawling across the still-warm, quivering mass in front of and slightly below him.

In a few minutes of groping he had a picture of what had dropped out of the dark sky, almost on top of him.

Two wolves. Both dead now, no signs of life, jaws slack, tongues lolling between naked teeth, eyes bulging.

There was a half-naked man's hand gripping each throat in a death-hold.

Between the lobos' bodies the man lay, bloody, clothes torn, cruciform in his unmoving sprawl, face and torso gashed by raking claws. There was a lot of blood on his neck. *A helluva lot.*

Tarne Shiels sat back, heart hammering.

'By God, Injun, you done for both of 'em – but they ripped your throat out while you was doin' it!'

At the same moment as he spoke he realized this was no Chiricahua brave.

It was a white man. Or what was left of him.

CHAPTER 2

NIGHT RIDERS

It was raining hard, unusually so for this part of the country, when the two slicker-clad riders appeared at the edge of Tarne Shiels's night camp.

The herd had been driven to the railhead and sold for a good profit and now Shiels and his crew were on the long trail home. Their mood was easy-going, if not down-right happy: full pockets and full bellies – a good combination.

The big tarp had been spread enough for the crew to set up their bedrolls and saddles, on which they sat while they spooned up a savoury stew. The two newcomers leaned their hands on their saddle horns just outside the firelit area, and Shiels, standing large and looking like some kind of patriarch with his fluffed-out muttonchop whiskers, lifted a fork in invitation.

'Step you down out of the wet, gents.'

The riders nodded and dismounted, leav-

14

ing the wet, weary mounts' reins to trail while they ducked under the sagging tarp's edge. The tall one was bearded and his eyes glittered darkly as he glanced around at the mildly curious trail crew.

'Smells good.'

'Be better still with some fresh biscuits,' griped his companion, shorter, broader, stubbled and moon-faced.

Shiels gestured to where the cook squatted over the fire arrayed with iron pots, his back to the company.

'Believe there's biscuits on the go right now.'

The strangers grunted, walked to a pile of tin platters. The tall one thrust a plate under the nose of the cook. He started when the man looked up from under a battered curl-brim hat. His face was marred by long, healing scratches. The edge of a dirty bandage showed under the hat, another above his collar. His hands were also bitten and scratched.

'Man, what the hell you been doin'? Wrasslin' a grizzly?'

The cook said nothing, dolloped two ladlefuls of stew on to the platter and the short man shouldered forward for his share.

'Them biscuits ready yet?' asked the tall

one, nodding towards a covered circular cast-iron trail oven with hot coals smoking on the lid. 'Shorty's got my mouth set for 'em now.'

The cook took a rag, gingerly lifted one edge of the lid and shook his head.

'Well, how long?' The tall rider sounded impatient.

The cook shrugged and the bearded face tightened but Tarne Shiels said, 'Be but a few minutes; he bakes well.'

Dark eyes swivelled to the trail boss. 'He a dummy?'

'We call him "Silent". Some Chiricahuas threw him to the wolves three weeks ago. Nigh tore out his throat, but he killed two of the dogs barehanded. Our Doc Jones patched him up. He's comin' along well.'

'He can't talk, then?'

'He can – in a kind of hoarse whisper but it hurts. Damn good cook. Set an' enjoy. You won't need conversation.'

The tall man continued to stare at the cook, the lean rawboned face, the jaw like a slab of iron, eyes that went right through a man. Standing, he figured the cook would be over six feet, lean, hickory-taut muscle all the way. In good shape for a lowly trail cook.

The rider hunkered down and started

eating the stew. He gulped it down, wiped the back of a hand across his mouth, and set down his platter beside his rock. 'Now for them biscuits, dummy.'

There was tension in the camp; a stranger rides in, is offered the civilities of a trail-camp on a wet night and speaks to the cook like that...?

Suddenly the tall man swore and began stomping wildly. His short companion chuckled as the other kicked a mangled rock lizard into the fire, where it sizzled.

'Now what in hell you do that for!' Doc Jones was standing before the seated tall man, his fists clenched down at his side, his young, trail-gaunt face tight with anger. 'First you leave your hosses standing in the rain, now – this. Lizard that size wouldn't do you no harm.'

'Doc, it's all right,' said Shiels softly and looked steadily at the tall man. 'Doc cares for every living thing, human or otherwise.'

'Yeah? Well, I don't care for no damn lizard runnin' across my hand and platter I gotta eat off.'

'There's the wash barrel.' Shiels pointed with his fork, face hard.

'Hell, dishwashin's the dummy's job.'

'Mister, if you've finished eating, you an'

your friend have a cup of java. Then you'd best be ridin' on.'

'They told me you were hard, Shiels.'

'You know my name?'

'Know more'n that.' The tall man swept his slicker back and let his hand rest close to the handle of his Colt. The short man stood slowly. 'Dummy. Gimme some biscuits. Now! I ain't waitin' any longer.' *Why was he being so damn provocative...?*

As he stepped forward Doc moved into his path. 'He's not a dummy.'

'That so? You ask me, the whole damn camp is full of dummies!' The tall man whipped out his Colt and slammed Doc across the side of the head. Doc collapsed and next moment the tall man was scream-ing as the trail-oven iron lid, scattering hot coals against him, bounced off his head and sent him staggering, hat flying wild. He spun towards the cook who was coming after the lid in a blur of speed. The gun came up and Silent took it from him easily. The short man triggered a shot which the cook ignored. There was a flurry of fists and the tall man, bloody-faced now, stumbled back, snatching at a hunting knife in his belt. Silent fired two shots and the tall man was flung backwards. The smoking barrel turned on the short man whose mouth was sagging in surprise. Silent shot him in the hip. He fell, screaming.

Most of the men were stunned by the sudden violence and speed of the action, especially from this man who had dropped out of the night with a dead wolf in each hand and half his throat torn out a few weeks ago and who had uttered barely a word since. Yet, doctored by young, caring Jones, after the trail cook was trampled in a stampede, the wolf-killer simply took over the dead man's chore and earned the undying gratitude of every ranny in Tarne Shiels's crew. They'd never had such good grub.

Now, the cook stood there with a smoking Colt in his hand, looking as if it was growing out of him; the gun seemed right at home in that scratched and torn fist.

Tarne Shiels stared. Then he asked, quietly, 'You've remembered something?'

Silent nodded, gestured to the dead man and the other who had passed out now.

In a rasping, hoarse voice, barely audible above the roar of rain on the overhead tarp, Silent said, 'They came to kill me.'

The dead man lay out in the rain all night; he didn't seem to mind.

Young Doc, head ringing from the gun-whipping, nonetheless treated the short one's shattered hip, tenderly and with as much expertise as he could muster.

'This one won't never walk without a stick.'

Silent stood by, watching, as Shiels packed his corncob pipe. 'He got a name?'

Silent shrugged, held the grimy bandage around his injured throat and winced as he swallowed. 'Just "Shorty" I guess.' It was a hoarse, phlegmy sound, the words difficult to make out. Shiels waited but Silent said no more.

'Not Law?'

Silent shook his head. Shorty stared up, past Doc's shoulder as the young ranny padded the wound before bandaging.

'Christ! Watch what you're doin'! That blame well hurts!'

'It'd hurt more if I had to take your leg off.'

Shorty paled quickly, greyness drawing his face into etched lines of pain. 'It – it that – bad?'

'You need proper medical attention. I'm an amateur. Never quite finished medical school.' Jones smiled crookedly. 'They said folk wouldn't want to deal with a doctor if they knew he'd killed one of his patients.'

Shorty's gaze sought the trail boss. 'That gospel?'

Shiels shrugged. 'We don't ask a man about his past. If he volunteers, that's up to him.'

'Boss, he'll lose that leg unless he gets to a proper doctor. We'll pass the swing-station north of Bisbee. I've got kin there, a half-sister. Wouldn't mind seeing her again. If it's OK with you, we can make a litter, a travois, for this ungrateful son of a bitch and I'll take him in. Might join up with you again later.'

'You're too soft, Doc, but it's up to you. Be damn sorry to lose you. 'Specially on account of scum like this.'

Jones started as he felt a hand touch his arm, looked surprised as Silent nodded. 'Me ... too.' He touched the throat bandage as he rasped the words. 'Saved my – life.'

'Enjoyed doing it, Silent. You remembered your name yet?'

Silent hesitated and then nodded. They waited and he croaked, 'I like "Silent".'

'So we can't put a name to you yet?'

Silent forced a smile, his wide mouth spreading, but not showing any teeth. 'My own name means trouble.'

Shiels sensed something here, a new restlessness in this strange man. He nodded. 'Your choice. You're welcome to ride all the way back to Nogales with us. Could even be in time to pick up another herd to end the season with. I'd have no trouble gettin' a crew if you was to stay on as cook.'

Silent shook his head. There was a pause as he made an inner effort so he could speak, and that told Shiels just how much it must hurt. 'Know what I have to do now.'

Shiels nodded and Doc said, 'You were lucky that fall didn't break your neck. Must say I'm kind of surprised you recollected. Memory loss for a month usually runs on into something more permanent.'

Tarne Shiels puffed on his pipe and watched Silent through the cloud of smoke. 'I owe you some money. Trail cook's pay as far as the railhead, and a home-goin' ticket. Anywhere particular you want it made out to?'

Silent held his gaze, shook his head slowly. He touched his bandages, indicating he had already been paid. 'Need a Colt, a rifle and a horse, though.'

Shiels grinned. 'Reckon you laid claim to the tall feller's gear. Yours for the taking – horse an' all. That roan looks good and I

22

reckon you'll treat it better'n he did. He have a name?'

Silent hesitated. 'Bowdrie – Bodine. Like that.'

'Silent, if there's help we can give...? I mean, you worked at cookin' when you were mighty poorly. Long hours. You've earned a helpin' hand if you need one.'

'Way he took care of them two night-riders he don't need no help,' spoke up Izzy, the wrangler, who was squatting nearby. 'An' I sure will miss your biscuits, if you cut out, Silent...' Izzy hesitated, then gestured to Shorty. 'Him an' his pard have ... friends?'

Silent nodded slowly. 'Would guess so.'

The wrangler swept an arm around the men still huddling out of the rain. 'Ain't a man here wouldn't be glad to stand by you, Silent.'

The wolf-killer – they had dubbed him 'Silent Wolf' in the camp – nodded, touched a couple of fingers to his hat brim in salute by way of thanks – but no, thanks.

He didn't need help. Didn't aim to ask for help – or plain didn't want it under any circumstances.

A lone wolf – *el lobo solo*...

'When?' Shiels asked, indicating the wind-and-rain-whipped night.

'Sun-up.'

'Wait till the rain eases. The river'll be high.'

'Makes no difference.'

Later, Shiels, checking the tension on the tarp ropes one last time before turning in, knelt beside Silent's bedroll. He saw the man's dark eyes swivel up towards him, sensed a hand moving slightly under the blanket – tightening his grip on the dead man's Colt he had inherited, maybe.

'Not tryin' to crowd you, but if there's big trouble, you call on us, any of us, any time. I've got a place outside Nogales. Nothin' fancy, lot of goddamn hard work, really, but I manage to feed and clothe a wife and three kids. Spare bed there for you any time. And an extra gun should you need one.'

Silent nodded, smiled slowly, lifted his right hand with its iodine-painted scratches and cuts, and gripped briefly with the trail boss.

His hoarse whisper was just audible. 'Them two,' Tarne Shiels knew who he meant, 'an' some pards, threw me to the Chiricahuas, figured they were done with me. Injuns ate my hoss, then tossed me to the wolves for some fun. I got a lot of ... settling to do.'

'Alone?'

'Only way I know.' He almost gasped the last words; talking obviously was still quite a strain for him.

Shiels squeezed Silent's shoulder, stood and made his way to his own bedroll.

Someone was going to rue the day – or night – they threw this one to the wolves.

CHAPTER 3

LONE WOLF

'If that throat wound begins to weep, see a doctor right away,' young Doc Jones had told him before he left the outfit. 'Keep it clean with the Eusol antiseptic and it'll dry up. Your voice'll return eventually.' The young medico grinned. 'Might not make the church choir, but...'

Silent's throat was sore. It hurt to swallow and ached nearly all the time. Fluids did little to soothe it. Jones had told him it was the muscle structure that caused most of the pain. It was all what he called 'outside' damage.

'Otherwise, you'd likely have little or no chance of ever getting your voice back. Good luck, *amigo*.'

Silent stayed on the wild trails for two days, always edging west, knowing where he wanted to go now, but he needed to be able to speak so he could ask questions. He bathed the throat wound twice a day in the evil-smelling antiseptic Jones had given him, rubbed in the salve, all without much improvement.

He made an abrupt decision when riding through saguaro and Joshua trees, all reminding him of grotesque human shapes in silhouette: he would head for St David, look up a sawbones, and start asking questions again.

Decision made, he pushed Bowdrie's roan harder now, heading into rough country, across the stubbly toboso grass, wanting to get to the town as quickly as possible.

There was a slow, good feeling deep within him now. After those weeks full of nightmare images, none of which made sense or formed any kind of sequence, suddenly it had all started to come back, a little at a time.

With the arrival of Shorty and Bowdrie – no, not their arrival – but damn soon after, when Bowdrie started acting up, picking on young, defenceless Doc Jones – it had returned in a surge, like a tidal wave he had read about once, engulfing everything. Except that he came through alive and his memory began to slot into place.

The missed rendezvous and the certain-sure

27

hunch that something had gone wrong. The long search. All the signs he dreaded. The man-count rising from two or three to a whole gang – six, seven, as many as ten, if he included those on the fringe – all somehow involved in Larry's death.

The men and the horror – the latter growing worse once they knew he was on their trail. The wolves and the Apaches had almost put an end to that and he would be forever obliged to Tarne Shiels and his crew: men to ride the river with.

And now he was on the trail again. Perhaps he ought to have questioned Shorty but the man was crazy with the pain of his shattered hip and Doc, in his non-discriminating humanity, had kept him in a kind of daze with doses of laudanum. No, he had to rely on himself now. *As always! El solo lobo* – The Lone Wolf, as Tarne had dubbed him.

Well, even a lone *lobo* could hunt and kill its prey successfully...

It was two hours after sun-up when he saw the low buildings smudging the grey-green land ahead, already shimmering in early heat. A small town, but busy. A few questions in the right place might gain him something here. He had been heading this way when they had caught up with him, realized he knew less than they did, so turned him over to the Chiricahuas, guns, horse and all.

Well, Bowdrie had paid for his part in the doings and Shorty would remember him for the rest of his life, with every dragging, crippled step he took.

And that suited him. There were others yet who would die, with his name a final curse on their bloody lips.

He stalled the roan in the livery, found his way to a sawbones who seemed sceptical of his story, but agreed to examine his throat.

'This was stitched by a professional.' There was mild accusation in the doctor's tone. He was a hawk-faced, grey-haired man, who had come out here for his lungs, which wheezed like leaky bellows. 'No trail hand did this!'

'Student,' Silent rasped.

'Then he has a damn fine medical future ahead of him. You've kept it clean and it's healing well. You have healthy flesh, mister, and those bites aren't infected. That'll be two dollars and thirty-five cents. I'll throw in another jar of salve and we'll call it two-fifty, even.'

Silent paid, knowing it was too much, but the relief of hearing the wound was healing was worth it. He went to a saloon, ordered minced veal pie – it hurt him to chew beefsteak – and a beer. The drink felt good going down. He ate slowly, aware of the curious stares of drinkers coming and going; a stranger in a place this size was sure to stir many questions. Especially bandaged and scratched-up the way he was.

Outside, he saw the San Pedro Stageline banner strung across the falsefront of a weathered building opposite. He crossed the street, carrying his rifle loosely in his left hand. Entering the office, he nodded to the bored clerk who was batting at flies with a rolled-up newspaper. The man didn't bother to get off his stool. The desk was a mess.

'No stages runnin' for two days. Rain in the hills has caused some washaways. Livery can hire you a mount if you're desperate to leave our bright lights.'

'I have a horse.' Silent's rasping words brought the man around sharply and there was actual interest on his stubbled face now. 'Heard you lost a stage couple of months back.'

The clerk was suddenly wary. 'We never lost it. Apaches attacked it. A massacre.'

'Passengers? Driver? Guard?'

'All killed. What's your interest?'

Silent stared hard and the clerk frowned as he dropped his gaze. Silent walked to the fly-specked map of southern Arizona on the wall. He tapped it with one iodine-yellow finger.

'Show me.'

'Listen, I don't have time for this. You got some kinda fever, the way you talk. We got a good sawbones if...'

Silent lifted his rifle on to the counter and the man stepped back, alarmed, boredom gone. 'Show me.'

It was enough. The clerk came round the counter, stood in front of the map, squinted and took off his half-moon glasses, started to polish them on a loose fold of his shirt. He sucked down a deep breath when Silent reached out, took the glasses from him and pushed them roughly back on the man's face, crooked but firm.

'Clean enough! And, mister, it hurts me to talk.'

The clerk swallowed, adjusted his spectacles and tapped a finger on the map. 'South of Benson. On the Tombstone part of the run. About... here. Bottom of a gulch, all choked with brush, greasewood and such. That's how come the search party missed findin' it for a few days.'

'Or it wasn't there when they first looked.'

The clerk blinked. 'Wha...? Aw, now how

31

could that be? It was off-trail, sure, but that was likely when they tried to outrun the Injuns. Sign was plain enough. Went clear off the edge.'

'Everyone aboard?'

'We-ell ... they found 'em scattered back up the draw. Driver closest. They'd cut his ears off, then shot him.'

Silent waited: *Apache renegades didn't kill their prisoners that quickly.* The clerk cleared his throat. 'The guard – they say he had hardly an inch of skin left on him. Them Apaches musta been mad with blood-lust. Drunk on rotgut tulapai or mescal–'

'They wanted something?'

'Dunno what. Was only a reg'lar run. Nothin' in the express box to get excited about. Mine records and a few packages. The big San Pedro mine is closin', out at Sahuarita. Lot of loner claims already shut down.'

'The stage passengers,' Silent reminded him bleakly.

The clerk looked uneasy. 'Look, I dunno as I oughta be talkin' to you like this.'

'Best you do.'

That rasp was getting on the clerk's nerves, backed by this tall waddy's dark eyes that looked like some kind of predatory animal's. His stomach was churning.

'Well, there was two women, one old, one ... twenties, I believe.' He shrugged. 'You know Injuns – wild blood up. Somethin' about a white woman when they got her at their mercy.' Silent waited and the man added in a low voice, 'Wasn't pretty...'

'Anyone else?'

'Two men. Mine manager, Pat Sievers, and another feller, dunno what his business was. Both dead.'

'Mutilated, too?'

'Not like... the guard an' driver.'

'Catch 'em?'

'The Injuns? Nah! Not a chance in that country. They do what they like out there. No white man can track 'em.'

'What'd they get from the stage?'

'Well, I guess they likely ate the team, them bein' partial to horseflesh. There'd've been a few guns. Some dresses for the squaws. All the harness, some gewgaws in the luggage, I guess, mebbe a bottle or two of whiskey. Wouldn't be bothered with any cash. That's about all, I'd say.'

Silent nodded. 'Not worth their effort,' he said flatly, turned, and walked out, making his way down the street through the warm sunshine to the livery.

He would go take a look at this draw

where the stage was supposed to have been attacked by renegade Apaches.

He nodded to the livery man working over his books in his cubbyhole office and turned into the stall where the roan munched on a nosebag. He slid the rifle into the saddle scabbard and rounded fast as a voice said,

'Nice-lookin' roan, that, with the pale mane and tail matchin' up thataway. Only other one I ever seen was owned by my brother. Or mebbe it was this one.'

The man who was talking was big, heavily built rather than tall, and broad; he looked like a rock wearing boots, and he held a Colt in his fist, pointed at Silent.

He also had a sidekick: a man about Silent's size, but with hair hanging down to his shoulders and wearing a fringed, grease-stained buckskin shirt. He cradled a carbine with casual menace in his bony arms. He nodded to his pard.

'Think you're right, Willie. That sure looks like Zack's roan to me.'

The broad man nodded, bleak, tobacco-coloured eyes boring into Silent. "Bout time you spoke up, mister.'

Silent touched the bandage around his neck, made his voice hoarser than usual. 'Hurts.'

The big man, Will, nodded. 'It'll hurt a lot more you don't talk. You got my word on that.'

The other man chuckled, moved the carbine, just reminding Silent he was under two guns.

Carefully, Silent lifted his hands across his shirt front towards his left-hand pocket, fumbling at the flap.

'Bill of sale.'

That surprised them both but Will recovered swiftly, jerked the Colt again. 'Let's see it.'

'Injuns got my hoss. Bought this one off a trail herd.'

Silent fumbled out a crumpled and grubby piece of paper, something Tarne Shiels had insisted he take. A fake bill of sale for the roan: *'Owner's dead. No one'll make out the signature anyway. Could save you some trouble. That mane and tail are unusual.'*

Now Silent was glad Shiels had thought of this. Will snatched the paper, frowned over it, waved it. 'Christ, looks like a fly crawled outta the ink bottle an' died right there.' Will stared a little longer, screwed up the paper and tossed it on the straw-littered floor, grinding it to shreds. 'It's a fake!'

'This Greener ain't!' a voice said from the

aisle and Silent moved his head enough to see the livery man standing there with a short, neatly dressed man who had a star pinned to his shirt pocket. He was holding a long-barrelled shotgun, covering Will and the other man.

'Like to see guns in leather in my town.'

Will hesitated but nodded and holstered his Colt. The lawman swung his eyes towards the lanky man, who lowered the hammer on his carbine and held it down at his side, muzzle pointing to the floor.

'Tate?' The lawman spoke to the livery man without taking his eyes off Will and his pard.

'Feller with the bandages rode in couple hours back, asked for a sawbones. He come back 'bout five minutes ago and these two stepped outta one of my stalls with guns. I seen you comin' outta the general store, Sheriff, an' figured if there was gonna be any trouble–'

'There won't be,' the lawman said, his look challenging.

'I'm Will Bowdrie. This ranny forkin' my brother's hoss, hands me a fake bill of sale.'

Sheriff Lyall looked quizzically at Silent who touched his throat bandages. 'Hurts to talk, Sheriff. But I can write you a statement.'

The lawman agreed and he gestured for Bowdrie and his pard to walk ahead, turn left and cross the street towards the tiny law office.

There, Silent wrote his statement. Sheriff Dan Lyall read it swiftly, his lips moving with each word.

'Basically, you were waitin' for the stage at Green Tanks. It never turned up; you went lookin' and run into some Chiricahuas who gave you a hard time and threw you to the wolves. But Tarne Shiels, who I know as a man to ride the river with, took you into his outfit and cared for you.' Lyall's eyes watched Bowdrie who kept his large face mostly blank.

'How'd he get Zack's hoss, Sheriff? That's what I want to know.'

The lawman returned to the paper. 'Says here he acted as camp cook for Shiels and took the roan as payment after they made railhead. You know where Shiels got the hoss, mister?' As Silent shook his head Lyall squinted at the paper. 'You ain't signed this!'

'Can't recollect my name. Hit my head when I fell off the cliff.'

'Now ain't *that* convenient!' growled Bowdrie.

The sheriff sat back in his desk chair, took

out a cheroot from the pocket that had the badge pinned to it and fired up. 'Because I know Tarne Shiels, I'll take your word about the bill of sale. Bowdrie, yours is a name I know, too. It's on a Wanted dodger in my drawer.'

'Not me!'

'No, your brother Zack. If, as you claim, the roan was his and he ain't around any longer...' Lyall spread his hands and Bowdrie swore softly. 'I got no argument with this feller.'

'You sayin' Shiels killed Zack?'

'If he did, he'd have a damn good reason. Like your brother was tryin' to rustle some of his stock – which is one of the things he was wanted for. Way I see it, best way to settle this is for you to leave things as they are.'

'Best way for who!' Bowdrie demanded.

His pard looked uncomfortable, nudged him, saying, 'Ain't nothin' we can do, Will. We've got the short end.'

'You can say that again!' Bowdrie glared. 'I ain't gonna forget this, Lyall!' Then he looked at Silent. 'Nor you, whoever the hell you are!'

'Remember all you want,' the lawman invited. 'Just do it outside of my town.'

Bowdrie didn't wait another second. He heeled so sharply he almost overbalanced, grabbed at his pard to steady himself and then stomped out.

'You're who?' Lyall snapped at the lanky man.

The man paused in the doorway. 'Woody Bigelow. An' you won't find no dodger with my name on it.'

'Which makes you lucky.'

When they had gone, Lyall turned to Silent. 'Wanna try again at rememberin' your name?'

'Been trying for a month. Tarne dubbed me "Silent".'

'Not acceptable. But you clear town and I won't have to bother you none.'

Silent stood, thrust out his scarred right hand. 'Obliged for you taking my part, Sheriff.'

Lyall made no effort to shake hands. 'I'll finish smokin' on the front landin'. Expect you to ride on by before I toss away the stub.'

Silent left.

As he paid the livery man, ready to mount, he rasped, '*Gracias, amigo* – for calling the sheriff.'

'You looked like you'd had trouble enough.'

'Feels like enough.'

The hostler grinned. 'Keep that sense of humour, you'll go far!'

Settling into leather, Silent looked down at the man. 'Need to go far enough to where they found that stage.'

'Ain't much left of it now: kids, looters, weather.'

'Apaches?'

'Not sure there ever was any 'Patchies – an' that's not just my opinion. Somethin' queer about it all. Stage was s'posed to go Benson, St David, Tombstone and points south, but it was sighted north of Huachuca City, 'way west an' south of where it shoulda been.'

'What would take it Huachuca way?'

The hostler shrugged, obviously uncomfortable with this conversation. 'Sourdough country. Old mines closed down, abandoned because they weren't producin' pay dirt.' He shifted from one foot to another. 'Feller couldn't pay his feed bill one time, figured to square me by givin' me what he called "privileged information". Said a couple them old mines'd been reworked by San Pedro: they sent someone down to look 'em over. If it showed promise they just walked in and started diggin'. No cost. A big company like San Pedro could afford to work a lean rockface long after a loner give up. This feller reckoned it was worth their while.' He paused and added quietly, 'Only they didn't know it...'

It was obvious Tate figured he had said enough –maybe more than enough.

If the mine was reported as 'dead' and the pay dirt never recorded, someone had himself a sackful of gold dust no one knew about.

Tate cleared his throat. 'Stage was way off route, tryin' to outrun the raiders, whoever they were. You ride seven mile south. Turn at a pink needle rock. Mile and a half on you'll find the draw an' what's left of it.'

He nodded curtly and Silent lifted a hand in farewell, rode out into the sunlight.

He saw Sheriff Lyall standing on his office landing, flicking away his cheroot stub, staring towards the livery, his flat shoulders angled impatiently.

Silent smiled to himself: the clock had been on him all right. Seemed Lyall was no man to fool with.

CHAPTER 4

KIN

The infirmary in Bisbee was down a side street on a corner. The name on the shingle above the rickety gate in the staggering picket fence said that this was the home and infirmary of Abel Farrow, MD.

He was a fat man, sweated a lot, had a head of wild grey hair and, although he looked a jolly type, was mighty serious with his patients. He and Doc Jones were washing up after making a plaster cast to immobilize Shorty's hip. The patient was snoring, the room reeking of chloroform.

'If you failed medical school, son, it's the profession's loss. Licence or not, you're a damn fine doctor.'

'Can't call myself that, sir. I – I made a bad mistake. Administered four grains of morphine instead of one quarter.' Farrow's fat lips pursed and his heavy eyebrows arched.

'That is – quite a large dose!'

'Fatal. College covered it up, made allowance because I had a heavy study load as well as a chest cold. I was dosed up with suppressants which affected my vision. But I – well, it was about as bad a mistake as any doctor could make.'

'So you quit. Well, boy, I could tell you of worse mistakes and no one ever got to hear about them. Instruments left in the body cavity, swabs, too. Filthy bandages reused on already infected wounds resulting in gangrene. Well, you'd have heard the stories. Not all fanciful, I'm afraid.'

'I wouldn't mind finding a small practice where I could assist. Work under supervision. That'd satisfy me.'

Farrow smiled thinly, not an easy thing to do with lips as rubbery as his. 'The area's beginning to fill up around Bisbee and Contention. I might be able to find room for a junior partner.'

Jones looked at him quickly. 'I wasn't hinting, sir, or trying to play on your sympathy.'

'I'd've shown you the door by now if I thought you were. Give it some thought, son. You say you have a half-sister in town. Go spend some time with her, come back later and we'll have us a talk.'

Jones slid his eyes to the bed where Shorty lay.

'He'll be all right. If he does what we tell him, he'll keep the leg. If he doesn't – well, the local Boot Hill is expanding with the population, too.'

Doc Jones's half-sister was named Gail Cobb and she did part-time dressmaking for the ladies of Bisbee when she wasn't working behind the drapery counter at Tellman's general store on Main.

Tellman was a hungry-looking man with a large hooked nose over a tight-lipped mouth, but he had a pleasant voice with a lightly bantering tone that was in contrast with his mournful appearance.

'And what can we sell you, young sir? You look as if you have long trails behind you. Perhaps in need of a new outfit?' He indicated Jones's shabby trail clothes and stubble.

Jones smiled. 'Sorry, Mr Tellman. It's me, Terry Jones...? I'm looking for Gail.'

Tellman lifted the spectacles dangling on a cord around his skinny neck, held them in front of his eyes without fitting them and nodded. 'Well, bless me! So it is! Are you a doctor yet?'

'Not ... quite, sir. Is Gail still working here?'

'Not today. I've given her a half-day off.' He leaned across the counter and spoke in a lower tone. 'There's some kind of hoedown Saturday night. You recall my eldest daughter, Lou? Yes, of course. Well, she's met this young attorney just setting up down the street and he's invited her as his partner.'

'And Gail's making Lou's frock?'

'That she is. She's moved since you were here last. Lives on Freeman Street now, little cottage on half an acre. I think she intends to extend and go into dressmaking full time.'

Well, that sounded like Gail: she was good at what she did, enjoyed working with fabrics. Maybe he would take up Doc Farrow's offer and he could help her get started in a full-time business.

She was taller than Jones, but they both had the same flax-coloured hair, a legacy from their mutual mother, although Gail had inherited her father's height while Jones seemed to have taken his mother's short stature.

She was pleased to see him though he thought he detected some sadness there behind the clear blue eyes. They gossiped lightly about their lives over the three years since they had last met.

In a lull, sipping his coffee, Jones asked, 'Your father still driving the stages?'

He knew it was a mistake. Her oval face lost its normal pleasantness, abruptly firmed into something he hadn't seen before; even the lovely eyes seemed suddenly to have shutters behind them.

'He's dead, Terry.' She watched his jaw sag in confusion, but gave him no time to speak. 'A couple of month ago. Indians attacked the stage he was driving to Tombstone, killed everyone aboard – some with horrible mutilations.'

'My God! I – I believe I heard about that!' He was thinking of Silent. 'We had a man come into our camp. He'd been attacked by wolves and I tended to him...'

'Naturally,' she said, with a faint smile now, reaching across the table to touch his hand. 'Mr Softy!'

He shrugged. 'He was in a fever on and off for a long time. He spoke of that stage. He'd been waiting for it at Green Tanks but it never turned up and he went looking for it. But Apaches got him and turned him loose in wolf country, for sport, I suppose.'

She was interested now, leaning across the table. 'He found the stage...?'

'I don't know.' Jones frowned as he looked

46

at her. 'It was strange; later, a couple of men came into camp and seemed to know Silent That's what we dubbed him, because he couldn't recall his own name and – well, there was trouble and this Silent killed one man and shot the other in the hip. I've just brought that one down to Dr Farrow for treatment.'

'This man who was killed ... Why was he interested in the stage?'

'It's – more an impression I got, Gail. A few things Silent said afterwards. Which were *very* few because he has this throat injury. He left Tarne's outfit to go to St David when I set out to come here.'

'St David!' She stood now and he was startled to see her small, fine-fingered hands clenching into fists at her sides. 'The stage was found near there! Miles off trail. It had been plundered, everyone ... slaughtered.'

'Sis! What's the trouble? Is it what they ... did to your father?'

Her eyes were filling now and she nodded jerkily, sat down slowly. She took a deep breath, bosom heaving, and clasped her hands. 'He was a good man, Terry. We were lucky, we both inherited Mother's lovely nature, but Lang Cobb was a good man.' She averted her eyes briefly. 'Not like your father – a drunkard who abandoned you and Mother.' She reached for his hand swiftly, squeezing out a smile. 'But you turned out to be a fine young man. Mother had some good years with Cobb before she died. Now he's dead – and – and – he didn't deserve to die the way he did!'

Jones sighed. 'Sis, Indian ways are savage by our lights, but they – well, they do the same kind of awful things to each other, you know. It's not just reserved for whites.'

'I don't care, Terry! I – I'm not satisfied with what was supposed to have happened to that stage. A lot of people aren't. There's talk it wasn't Indians at all, but white renegades.'

'Aw, now, sis, there's always that sort of gossip.'

She shook her head vigorously. 'No! I've spoken with the army captain who investigated and he wrote a report saying it was very suspect – but it was rejected, covered up. Because they *want* people to stay hostile to the Apaches! It's – it's bothered me for weeks, Terry. Cobb was very good to me, bought me this cottage. I owe it to him to learn the truth.'

'Gail, what're you talking about?'

'You know I'm a good horsewoman and I

can shoot well enough–'

'Oh, for heavens' sake, girl! You're not thinking of – of *doing* something? Investigating on your own! Now, you know that's ridiculous and, if there *are* white renegades involved, why, it'll be the most dangerous thing!'

'Tell me about this man you call "Silent", Terry,' she interrupted quietly and that hard, determined look was back, firming her beautiful features. 'It sounds as if he knows something...'

'She's determined to go, Doctor Farrow! I can't find any way to stop her.'

Jones was standing at the end of the bed where Shorty lay, half-asleep, moaning occasionally.

'Well, she is a determined young woman, son – competent, too. I've seen her riding. And she won the last turkey-shoot we held! Upset Blake Dempsey, the former champion, no end, being beaten by a woman. So much so that he eventually left town.'

'What can I do, sir? I can't let her ride into danger!'

'I see no way you can stop her, son. The best thing for you is to help Gail prepare for her ... venture, then come join me as my junior partner. Admit it, son. You'll never get past her stubbornness if she's already made up her mind to go find this "Silent" fellow at St David.'

Jones sighed again and nodded. He knew the older man was right; his sister *was* as stubborn as all get-out. She got that from *her* father.

After the men had left and Farrow's nurse was giving Shorty a quick sponge because of the heat, the man said, gritting his teeth a little against the endless pain in his hip:

'That kid brother of yours – the one who fetched me tobacco yes'ty.'

'And for which you paid him two bits! You'll spoil that boy!'

Shorty forced a smile. 'Tell him I want him to send a wire for me down at the telegraph office. He does it quick, I'll pay him a quarter.'

Silent reined in on the broken rim of the draw, looking at the black-scarred brush and the few remaining charred frames, heat-twisted iron wheels: all that was left of the stagecoach. It had been the usual Concord vehicle, he guessed as he eased the roan in a slow zigzag down the steep slope. There was little remaining but he climbed down and kicked some of the ashes here and there, found nothing helpful. Moving away out into the blackened greasewood and chaparral, he felt something crunch under his boot.

Broken glass, heat-blackened and cracked. There was a curled corner of a label on one piece, a little printing still showed through the dirt and scorch marks.

Part of an 'a' followed by an 'l'. Underneath, another 'l'.

It didn't take a genius to know this was from a bottle that had once contained coal oil. He looked around him slowly. Seemed to Silent there had been no attempt to extinguish the fire: it had just been allowed to burn.

Someone figured it was fun to watch – or it was lit to destroy evidence...

That was the rub. Kids could have done this, set fire to the remains just for the devilment of it. If he hadn't found the broken glass he might even have considered the fire had been accidental, some curious rider lighting a cigarette just before moving on, flicking the match carelessly into the greasewood. He wouldn't bother trying to extinguish the fire when there was only the wreckage of an old coach and a patch of brush to burn.

Suppose it had been deliberate, so as to destroy any possible evidence? But of – what?

It had mostly been accepted that Apaches or renegades had pursued the coach, the driver cutting off the regular trail in desperation, hoping to find help in little St David – but the stage simply hadn't made it.

Silent had scouted the broken rim of the draw before coming down here. Winds and morbid sightseers had mangled any sign that might have told whether the stage had gone over full tilt, or if it had been stopped short of the draw and later was *pushed* over the edge.

Well, he wasn't going to find out anything now, not after all this time. But he still scouted around, feeling the heat of the sun growing, burning through his shirt. He tugged at the throat bandage, the sweat trickling across his traumatized skin beneath. It wasn't quite so sore and tender to touch now – that was something.

'Figured you might show up around here sooner or later.'

The voice came from above him and Silent went down to one knee, twisting, hand slapping the butt of the holstered Colt. Glare on the rim gave him only a brief glimpse of someone standing there with a rifle – but he recognized the voice from the livery: Will Bowdrie.

Brush crackled to his left and he snapped his head around. Woody Bigelow stood in the shade of the rock slope, his carbine menacing, hammer spur drawn back under his thumb.

'We'll pick up where we left off,' Bigelow said conversationally. 'Or you still claimin' you can't speak?'

'Still.'

Bigelow chuckled. 'Hear that, Will?'

'I heard. And I guarantee he'll be sayin' *somethin'* before long. Mostly, *"Stop! Stop! I'll tell you!"*'

'Tell you what?' Silent rasped as Woody kept him covered while Bowdrie picked his way down the slope.

'See? He can talk, Will!'

Bowdrie was breathing slightly harder than normal as he reached the bottom of the draw and walked up to Silent.

'Sure, you can talk. An' you'll do a lot more talkin'. But you'll say what I want to hear or that nickname they gave you will be all they'll carve on your headboard!'

Silent knew what to expect but wasn't quite ready for Bowdrie's sudden lunging stride that put the man within reach. A gun barrel knocked Silent's hat off as he ducked just a mite late. Bowdrie snarled a curse and swung the rifle backhanded.

Silent was faster this time. It never touched him and he came up inside the swinging arm, drove a fist into Bowdrie's thick midriff. The man grunted and stopped in his tracks, staggering. Silent whipped two fast punches into the man's face, rammed a shoulder under the large-boned jaw, and lifted fast. He was taller than Bowdrie and the heavy man's teeth clacked together with a sound like a hammer driving a nail. The big head jerked back and Bowdrie's legs buckled. As he started to go down, Silent lifted a knee into his face and was following through with a clubbed fist to the back of the neck when Woody Bigelow stepped in and slammed the butt of the carbine against Silent's head.

He folded instantly, sprawling half on his side. Woody stood over him but was shoved roughly aside by the stumbling, bloody-faced Bowdrie. He drove a boot brutally into Silent's ribs, and another, this one hard enough to lift Silent a few inches off the ground.

Bowdrie spat some blood, wiped the back of a hand across his oozing nostrils and bared his teeth as he drew his Colt and cocked the hammer, aiming at the downed man's head.

'Will, don't!' snapped Bigelow. 'Kill him an' we'll never know for sure how much he knows!'

Bowdrie's burning eyes seemed slightly out of focus and Woody stepped back hurriedly, for an instant afraid the man was going to put a bullet into *him*. Then, slowly, some kind of sanity returned to Bowdrie and he spat out a curse, kicked Silent again, breathing hard.

'Son of a *bitch!*'

Woody tucked his carbine under his arm and took out tobacco sack and papers. He rolled a cigarette and handed it to Bowdrie, who took it, jammed it between his split lips. Bigelow held a match for him, then made himself a smoke and fired up.

'He's gonna be tough to crack,' Bigelow ventured at last, earning a steely glare. 'I mean, any man who can take what the 'Pachies did to him, then kill a couple wolves with his bare hands and falls off a cliff – *and* walks away – well, he ain't no Sunday-school teacher.'

'Zack was tryin' to kill him, so he musta figured he'd got outta him all he was gonna.'

'Zack was meaner'n you are, Will.' Bigelow said it slowly, tentatively, nerves ready to send him jumping out of reach, bringing the carbine out from under his arm fast enough to stop Bowdrie in his tracks. 'You're both hot-headed, move before you think, worry about consequences later.'

Bigelow's heart was hammering, but he made himself hold Will's angry gaze: it was time someone pulled the Bowdries into line. Otherwise no one was going to get anything at all out of this deal: not a damned plugged nickel.

CHAPTER 5

CAPTIVE

Maybe because Silent had had such a battering earlier and was in a coma for so long after his fall from the cliff, Woody's blow to the back of his head left him unconscious for a longer time than would be expected.

He didn't know how long, but when he started to come round it was dark and he had no idea where he was. *Seemed to be a lot of that lately!*

His wrists were tied with rawhide behind his back. His head thundered – no other word would fit, unless it was 'exploded'. His brain felt loose within his skull and the skull itself was one massive ache, burning down into his neck and shoulders. He could see but not very clearly, which might have been because of the lack of light: he hoped so, anyway. He couldn't bear the thought of going blind.

A footstep. Behind him. He tried to

wrench around but something in his neck clunked! several times and pain shot up into his head. He got a partial look, saw he was in some kind of shallow cave, facing the back wall – which explained how he was having difficulty orienting himself. Now, over his shoulder, he could see a light greyness in the form of a ragged-edged arch: the cave entrance, he guessed. Beyond was a small campfire. There was a man sitting on a log, gnawing on some kind of animal bone, likely a rabbit leg judging by the size.

But closer, there was a man standing in the entrance, something metallic glinting in his hand down at his side.

'Comin' round at last. Was gettin' kinda worried. Will thought he'd killed you.'

Silent said nothing and Woody Bigelow squatted down, felt the thongs to make sure Silent hadn't been trying to get loose. 'Want some java?'

The very word set Silent salivating. He nodded.

'You'll have to answer. Had a bellyful of this "silent" stuff. You can talk. If it hurts, so what? You *don't* talk and it'll hurt a helluva lot more. You been told.'

'Like some – coffee.' His throat ached like hell, but his mouth was so dry his tongue was sticking to the roof. His neck felt mighty sore but his throat seemed a little better. *No need to let on, though.*

Woody dragged him outside by his shirt collar, dumped him alongside the log where Bowdrie sat. He propped him up, splashed some steaming black coffee into a battered tin mug and held it to Silent's lips. It burned and he jerked his head back, the coffee spilling down his shirt front and scalding his chest.

Will Bowdrie laughed, placed a boot against Silent's shoulder and pushed him down on the ground. Woody cursed, shaking the hand the hot coffee had splashed. He nudged Silent roughly in the ribs.

'No coffee, damn you!' As if it was the prisoner's fault it had spilled and burned him.

'Hungry,' Silent grated, figuring he had nothing to lose – and the smell of the broiling jackrabbit was filling his mouth with saliva.

'And you'll stay that way,' growled Bowdrie. 'Till you decide to tell us what you know.'

'About – what?'

Will growled and kicked him again but Bigelow stepped in before the heavy-set man lost his temper.

'He don't get it yet, Will. Do you, dummy?'

Silent said nothing, trying to think through the headache and his throbbing body. *It was the stage, of course.*

'Dunno what you – want.'

Bowdrie thrust his big face close to Silent's. 'Why were you waitin' for the stage at Green Tanks? It ain't a reg'lar pick-up spot.'

'Was told it was comin' from Tucson and it'd be watering there. Thought I could – get a lift.'

Bowdrie and Bigelow exchanged a look. Woody arched his eyebrows and nodded slightly: *could be.*

But Bowdrie didn't want it to be that easy.

'Why you want to catch that stage?'

'Get to – Tombstone.'

Bowdrie kicked him again. 'Why, damnit? I gotta keep askin', you're gonna lose a helluva lot of hide.'

To back up his words, Will Bowdrie reached to the back of his belt and showed Silent a broad-bladed hunting-knife with a drop point. 'How much you reckon the gov'ment'd pay for your scalp?'

Silent said nothing but he wasn't surprised at the hint that Bowdrie had done some bounty hunting for Apache scalps. He seemed the kind of scum who would do that, sewing together a couple of kids' scalps to make it look like an adult one, which was worth more. Maybe wise, too, in the Indian ways, so he could even make a stage wreck look as if it had been attacked by genuine Apaches.

Silent went very still as he felt the edge of the blade touch his flesh slightly below the hairline. He sucked in a sharp breath and Bowdrie laughed; he liked that involuntary symptom of Silent's body's reaction to sudden, unbidden fear and threat.

'Someone told you about the gold, din' they?' Woody said, not quite at ease like Bowdrie with the threat of Indian-style killing.

'Gold?'

Bigelow kicked Silent this time. 'Don't stall!'

Silent's deadly eyes glittered in the re-flected firelight as he sought Woody's face. 'What'll you do? Flay me like the shotgun guard?'

Woody and Bowdrie exchanged a glance and big Will chuckled, kicking Silent in the chest, pinning him to the ground with his big boot and the weight of his leg.

'So you know about that, huh? I was right,

Woody, all along. This sonuver knows the deal! Anglin' for what he can get!' He shuffled off the log, hunkering down beside the prisoner now, placing the blade against the throat bandages.

Silent gasped as the cloth was slit and fell away from the wound. Bowdrie peered more closely.

'Say, them wolves sure did rip you up, huh! Zack thought they'd finish you. We got us a real tough ranny here, Woody. Feel able to rise to the challenge?'

Bigelow chuckled, now more at ease that he, too, was convinced Silent could tell them what he knew.

'Why don't we get us a good night's sleep, Will? We been trailin' for days. An', dunno about you, but I have trouble makin' out what he says. Leave him be for now and we'll mebbe buy him a cup of coffee, even a hunk of cold rabbit breast in the mornin', then get down to our powwow.'

'I wanna know who told him about the gold!'

Bowdrie wanted to push on and get it finished. But Woody insisted that too much strain on Silent's throat might make it all unintelligible and they'd have to make him write it out.

'An' we got no paper – not even a pencil.'

'All right, all *right!*' growled Bowdrie eventually. 'We got time, I guess. Been weeks already. They off-loaded that gold someplace and it'll still be there.' He leaned down and drew the blade lightly down the left side of Silent's face, opening a shallow scratch that barely bled. 'Now, I started that just under your eye. If I have to do it tomorrow, it'll be with the blade *in your eye.'* He laughed loud and stood up. 'Pleasant dreams, dummy!'

On the last word he punched Silent in the face. The prisoner lay there, unmoving, brain buzzing, tasting blood. Whatever lay ahead wouldn't be anything to look forward to.

But he had learned something: there *had* been gold on that stage at some time and these two had been kept in the dark about what had happened to it: they had helped rig things so it looked like the stage had been attacked and robbed, only they didn't know where the gold had been moved to before that. The trouble was, they thought he did.

He didn't get much sleep.

It wasn't just the pain; Bowdrie and Bige-low had a bottle of tequila or mescal and they began swigging in turns. There was lots of talk, dirty jokes, trying to outdo each other with their tales of women they had known – or said they had. Bloodier tales of using their knives, too...

The drunker they got, the more vicious they became when they noticed Silent lying there, trussed like a turkey, hands numbed and painful, his arms burning all the way up to his shoulders. He took several hard boots in the body, faked unconsciousness once or twice, but soon learned it didn't work with these two.

And then they started in on him in earnest until, in the end, he did lie there unconscious – no faking. Sometime during the night he woke and realized the camp was quiet and still except for the usual wilderness night sounds. One of them coughed and he thought the man might have retched in his sleep. Later, snores began mingling with the night sounds.

Painfully, he hitched his buttocks around the cave mouth where they had left him, worked his way to the lower edge on the left side of the arched entrance. He had noticed earlier that the rock had been split into layers when the entrance had formed, some kind of geological slip, leaving some flat planes of rock – with jagged edges.

Unfortunately, the rock was shale-like, soft. The edges crumbled easily. He twisted his tortured body so he could rub the rawhide thongs on these edges, felt them fracture and break away almost at once. Gasping, throat aching worse than usual – probably from thirst as much as anything else – he silently cursed, but forced the thongs back and rubbed again. Twice more the rock just disintegrated and then he felt a more solid portion that made him gasp as it raked his wrist, drawing blood.

He had crumbled away the outer, weathered layer; underneath was the more solid core.

He didn't know how long it took before he felt some give in the rawhide, but he was near exhaustion with his efforts. His back and shoulders and upper arms were solid bars of agony. He was gasping for breath so desperately that he was afraid the sounds might waken the killers.

But they slept on, snoring, coughing, not moving much: too drunk to be disturbed by such small sounds.

Bueno! His dazed mind roared inside his head. The first thong broke so suddenly that he fell on to his side and he had to struggle to get into position again. It was easier now, the bonds falling loosely away from his wrists.

His teeth sank into his lower lip, drawing blood, as circulation surged excruciatingly through arms and shoulders and fingertips. It was some time before he could even bring his hands around to his front where he tried to rub one with the other. It was not successful and he just sat there, trying not to moan aloud as the tingling feeling gradually increased and the raw pain slowly – very slowly – receded.

He looked around as he waited for relief. Near where Bigelow slept he saw what looked like his Colt and rifle propped on a saddle that he recognized as the one that had been on the roan.

Now he had to make his decision; did he get his weapons and kill these sons of bitches where they lay – or did he find the roan, saddle up while they slept drunkenly, and light out...?

He *wanted* to kill them, but he needed more information to make sure he had got the right ones. And he had learned enough to know that these two seemed to be only hired guns, but they could still lead him to the ones who did the hiring.

When he had first set out on this self-imposed chore he knew what he had to do. Killing was part of it, a big part of it, but there was something else, too.

He couldn't come to terms with the fact that innocent men and women had already died because of the smuggling of gold aboard that stage, died horribly and painfully. So, simply put, he could not allow their deaths to be in vain. They would be avenged, eventually, but, meantime…

He looked down at the sleeping beauties, trigger finger itching. 'All right,' he rasped aloud, adding to himself:

So you two have gotten yourselves a reprieve … but that's all it is – because you're both dead men walking.

CHAPTER 6

ALLY

Just for the hell of it, Silent ran off Bigelow's and Bowdrie's mounts.

He saddled the roan with a minimum of trouble; the few snorts it gave and the clink of its shoes as it pranced once or twice were nowhere near enough to disturb the sleeping killers. Ground-hitching the roan, he quickly and expertly made rope hackamores for the other horses, unhobbled them, and climbed into his saddle.

He led the mounts way down the draw, well out into the mesquite and chaparral, and hobbled them again. The brush was high enough to hide them from a cursory glance and by the time Bigelow and Bowdrie had staggered this far, they would be sweating and weak and cursing, literally floundering. *Good!*

Feeling lifted by the childish, though practical prank, he rode to the rimrock, turned back up the draw and found a way down in the northern reaches. The stars were bright now and the cusped moon sat atop the sawtooths, shedding light enough for him to see.

There was little he could find right now. There were a few places that tightened his lips, where he guessed the bodies of the passengers, driver and guard had been found, particularly the guard – there was a large spread of some dark stain on the ground. It had to be old blood.

If he had hoped to find something new that would confirm his suspicions he was disappointed.

Daylight was not far off and he backed the roan into a crevice, ground-hitched it and lay down on his blanket, surprised and not a little annoyed to find how tired he was. Still, he had taken a deal of punishment lately. Common sense prevailed and, although he felt the urge to be up and about, he opted for a sleep that would refresh him.

When he awoke, the sun was at least an hour in the sky – and a rifle was poking him roughly in the ribs, which were already sore and bruised, thanks to Bigelow and Bowdrie.

He pushed back his hat, threw up a hand so it cast a shadow over his face. Startled, he sat up quickly, wincing as pain shot through him and his brain seemed to slop around inside his skull.

'And just what're you doing here, mister?'

It was a woman's voice and he shifted slightly – so did the rifle barrel, following his every movement. He wanted to get a good look at her, saw she was tall, slim, with flaxen hair hanging to just above shoulders which were pretty broad for a woman. She was wearing a buckskin vest beautifully embroidered with entwining flowers and vines down the front, over a blue-striped blouse, and corduroy trousers.

Neat, feminine, and practical.

He noted, too, the .38 Smith & Wesson pistol in the holster high on her right hip, each loop of the narrow belt filled with a shiny brass cartridge.

'You look loaded for bear, miss,' he said and saw her start at his raspy voice. He massaged his throat and realized he had not replaced the bandage that Bowdrie had cut away. He would put on a bandanna later – if there was a 'later', and of that he was not too sure, the way she was looking at him now. She held the rifle easily and competently.

'What's your name?' she demanded bossily.

'They call me "Silent".'

The small frown stood out between her

eyes because of the low angle of the sun. 'Silent – Wolf?'

It was his turn to show surprise now and he nodded.

'You know a stubborn young man who goes by the name of "Doc" Jones?'

'Sure. He tended my throat – and the rest of me.'

She paused, as if making up her mind, then said, 'He's my half-brother. I'm Gail Cobb. He brought in a man shot through the hip to our medico in Bisbee. I believe it was you who shot that man: "Shorty" some-one.'

'Doc OK?'

'Yes. The local medic has offered to take him in as a junior partner. He'll never be licensed, but he'll be able to practise medicine under supervision.'

She hadn't yet swung the rifle away from him and he saw the hammer spur was still under her small thumb. He gestured to the weapon. 'He'll be good at whatever he does – and that rifle's so close I can smell the gun oil.'

She smiled. 'I keep my weapons clean and tuned.' But she lowered the hammer and let the gun swing to one side. 'Terry – that's Doc's real name in case you didn't know –

thinks a great deal of you, Silent. He's told me something about you, as much as he knows, I guess, but I'm sure there must be a lot more.'

Silent lived up to his nickname and she frowned.

'Am I prying?'

He stared back.

'All right – I'm sorry. But still curious.' Waiting did no good at all: he didn't explain anything. She sighed. 'My original question stands: what're you doing here?'

'Came to look at the stagecoach but two hardcases jumped me ... Will Bowdrie and Woody Bigelow.'

'Those two! They're well-known around Bisbee. Bullies, troublemakers, drunk most of the time. Guns for hire. Always manage to stay one jump ahead of the law.'

He was rubbing his aching throat again now. 'Well, I've made a few mistakes since I fell off that cliff.'

'Ye-es. With a dead wolf in each hand! My God, you must be a whole lot tougher than you look!'

'Aw, I've been sick,' he rasped, deadpan, whining.

She smiled slowly. 'I shouldn't've said that. I'm sorry. From what Terry said, you've been through a dreadful ordeal. And you're certainly no powder puff if you shot Zack Bowdrie.' She gave him a sharp look. 'I guess you know by now what mean types Will Bowdrie and Bigelow are?'

He nodded slowly. 'The stage guard was flayed alive. I've put that down to those two. And Zack.'

Her breath hissed in through white teeth and he thought a little blood drained from her handsome face. 'There was talk of some torture but I – never knew that.'

'Would it've stopped you coming?'

Her eyes narrowed. 'Not that – or anything else!' She drew a deep breath. 'You don't know why I'm here!'

He shrugged, held her gaze which had some anger in it now. Tight-lipped, she told him, 'I rode the stage overnight up from Bisbee, hired a mount when I heard you'd been in St David and later left. I took a chance on your coming here; I wanted to talk with you.' She paused, then snapped suddenly, 'What d'you intend doing now you've seen the stage?'

'First, see if you've got food.'

'I have. We'll breakfast shortly. Then...?'

'I have an agenda.'

'Which doesn't include me?'

He shook his head.

'I – believe you are a lot – tougher than I gave you credit for.' Her compliment had no visible effect on Silent. 'The driver of the coach was my father – Lang Cobb.'

Silent's face showed some interest at that. He thought of the stageline agent saying the attackers – Indians or whoever – had sliced the driver's ears off, then shot him. He didn't know if she had this information but he decided to be careful and not enlighten her – just in case it produced some un-expected reaction. Although, privately, he figured she was pretty tough, too: *pretty*, and pretty tough.

She sat down on a log, resting the rifle within easy reach, and began to rummage in her saddle-bags, bringing out cloth-wrapped cold food which she shared with him. Bis-cuits, cold beef which she thoughtfully sliced into thin slivers for him with a small hunt-ing-knife, cold corn patties and some salt. There was canteen water to drink.

They ate in silence, she watching him wince each time he swallowed.

'It must've been – terrifying, all those wolves attacking in the dark.'

'Dark's what saved me. I could hear them trying to find my scent. I was about to climb down the cliff when two came at me together and we all fell off the ledge.'

It was the longest speech he had made in weeks and he worked his jaws, surprised at the intensity of the ache the effort caused. She was studying him and suddenly said,

'Your real name – would it be "Clay"?'

He stiffened and that was answer enough.

'The stagecoach guard – his name was Larry Clay. He was younger but looked a lot like you do – under all that dirt and the scratches. I saw him in the express office in Bisbee.'

After a while he nodded. 'I'm Aaron Clay. Larry was my kid brother.'

'He was very young.' She chopped off the words and he knew she had been going to say something along the lines of 'to have died so horribly.'

'Yeah. Barely out of his teens. He took on the job as shotgun guard just for the Tombstone run. Needed the money, but he had no experience.' He frowned. 'Wondered why they hired him.' He had her full attention now. He hesitated and then, over the next few minutes, with frequent pauses and swills from her canteen, he told her how he and Larry planned to meet in Tombstone, get an outfit together and try prospecting the Dragoons.

'It was Larry's idea.' He smiled gently. 'He was a dreamer and had come by a "map" of a "lost" gold mine. Cost him five dollars. Very proud of himself.'

'He was cheated! You can buy those things for a drink and a dollar in any town along the border.'

'Yeah. Larry was a greenhorn, but he tried hard; desperate to join me out here. Figured it was man's country. Didn't want to discourage him.' *He'd had some growing-up to do and Silent had figured this was as good a place as any for it – under supervision – his.*

'You must've got along well – not all brothers do.'

Silent nodded. He had paid for Larry's schooling, such as it was, and the kid had done well. Was smart at figures and earned himself enough to pay his fare West by some part-time bookkeeping. The map probably wasn't the first time he was cheated out of hard-earned cash but he was so enthusiastic about joining his big brother that Silent didn't have the heart to discourage him.

Anyway, the experience would do him good and the kid could always fall back on his accounting skills if the prospecting didn't work out. Besides, Silent – *Aaron Clay* – had the reputation for taking chances, too, and he was willing to give Larry his chance: it was possible (but not likely, he admitted to himself) that the map just might lead to a workable vein of gold. In any case, it would be good to have the kid with him, working alongside, successful prospectors or not. That's what he'd thought: and he knew Larry had held a similar dream...

But Larry's enthusiasm, his efforts to pay his own way, had ended that dream...

The dream that would now turn into a nightmare for the men who had shattered the kid's hopes – and ended his life.

A goddamned living nightmare! He would see to that.

By the end of the day he felt he had known Gail Cobb for a long time.

She was friendly, open, spoke her mind, sometimes too quickly, and had the grace to blush and stammer an apology: he liked her. When he pressed her she told him she was a good rifle shot and he read between the lines – make that *excellent.* Without boasting, she occasionally dropped details of some of the turkey-shoots and competitions she had won around Bisbee and beyond. *Target shooter, though – different when your sights are on a man who might shoot back…*

'You want the men who killed your father,' he decided as they rode through a narrow pass.

She was slightly ahead and to one side of him, twisted to give him a sober look, the sun turning her flaxen hair to spun gold under the narrow-brimmed hat. 'I'm his only surviving kin. He was good to my mother – and to me.'

Silent nodded in understanding. 'Did you know there was talk of a secret gold shipment on board the stage?'

She nodded. 'But it must've been hidden well, if there was. There were rumours afterwards – but most folk just put it down to that: gossip. You saw what was left of the stagecoach. If it was there at all it must've been in the express box.'

'That's been found – still locked. Full of old mining reports and other papers. No gold.'

She frowned. 'Then it must've been hidden in the framework of the stagecoach, somehow. Perhaps in the roof lining or somewhere. If it existed, of course.'

'More likely off-loaded someplace along the line – labelled something else, something heavy because it would weigh plenty.

Be good to get a look at a few lading bills.'

She reined down, dropping back alongside him, even though the trail was narrow and dangerous now, above a sluggish stream. 'I never thought of that.'

'Possibility.' He was wearing his neckerchief now and ran a finger around the inside, letting some air against his lacerated, though healing skin.

'It must've been well-camouflaged.' She dropped a hand to the butt of her rifle in the scabbard under her leg. 'We should look for Bowdrie and Bigelow. They ought to have found their mounts by now.'

He nodded, pointed to a ledge above. 'We can watch from up there.'

'Ye-es. I could get in a good shot from that height.' He knew she spoke spontaneously, hadn't really thought about what she was saying.

'No. We follow them.' At her sharp look, he added, 'They'll lead us to the others.'

'Others?'

'I've been hunting 'em for weeks. A whole gang. Reckon there could be as many as eight or ten.'

Her jaw dropped slightly. 'My God! I thought it was just the Bowdries and Bigelow, with maybe one other! You're sure?'

'No. Just putting together a few things.'

'Why would they need so many for a simple holdup?'

'Not simple. If there really was a secret gold shipment, information had to come from inside.'

'The mining company? But the San Pedro has an excellent reputation!'

'But it's closing – worked out. Last chance for someone to get some easy money. Fake a hold-up along the way. Take gold, split it up later.'

She thought about it as they climbed slowly towards the ledge. It was possible, she allowed. *One last chance!* A lot of men would lose their jobs when the San Pedro Mining Company went out of business – from management to the lowliest mine-face grubber, freighters, timber-getters for the shaft shoring poles, the dynamite experts. A *lot* of men would be out of work, with little prospect of getting a comparable job. San Pedro wasn't the first big mine to close – even some of the original silver mines were struggling: a couple had already set up elsewhere, others, at considerable expense, had brought in geologists and mining experts from the bigger towns, scouring the Dragoons and adjacent hills for new payable lodes, underground water to be tapped for sluices. And some might even have checked out abandoned loner claims...

'Would there have been much gold? I mean, if the mine was closing...?'

'Not sure. From what I've heard, most mines always keep a reserve as back-up.'

'You've given this a great deal of thought, haven't you?'

He merely looked at her.

'My God!' she exclaimed suddenly. 'Your brother. That's what's driving you, isn't it? You're not interested in any gold!'

'Only if it'll point me to Larry's killers.'

He thought she gave a small, involuntary shudder. There was a new wariness in her now. 'You – you have a reputation? With a gun, I mean?'

'Not around here.'

'But somewhere. I'm thinking you shot Zack Bowdrie, a known gunfighter... Should I ask which side of the law you're on?'

'Wouldn't bother.'

This time her eyes widened and he smiled thinly as she unconsciously put a little more space between them, Gail easing back slightly so she could watch him better.

'There's the ledge,' he said but she didn't answer.

Suddenly, she had a great deal to think about.

And now she felt ... uneasy ... with this tall man and his strange, husky voice.

Not to mention his wolf-scarred face and the cold, deadly look that filled his eyes when he was talking about catching up with his brother's killers.

She was glad that they were allies: she sure wouldn't want Aaron Clay – or Silent Wolf – for an enemy.

CHAPTER 7

WOLVES GATHER

Bowdrie and Bigelow had found their mounts – at last. They were both in filthy moods – and a filthy state, clothes in rags, faces and hands scratched, the run-over riding boots taking their toll on aching feet and legs.

When they eventually located the horses, hobbled and browsing on the brush simply because there was nothing else, they found Silent had left them with no hackamores. Now there was nothing to lead or control the animals with: the hobbles weren't long enough to convert. It meant climbing aboard, bareback, only the manes to hold – and range mounts soon tired of such tension on *those*, and soon let the rider know it.

'I'm gonna slice that son of a bitch into pieces small enough to feed to a snake!' Will Bowdrie vowed, hawking and holding a hand to his forehead.

'Have to find him first,' muttered Woody Bigelow, settling uncomfortably on his uncooperative mount.

'I'll find him! If it takes the rest of my life!'

'Unless he finds you first.'

'Why would he look for me now? He's had his fun!'

'I got me a bad feelin' about that *hombre*, is all. Anyways, I reckon Ralls knows where the gold is all along. This chore he's sent us on is just a blind, get us outta the way so eventually we're left holdin' the bag – an *empty* bag!' He licked his lips. 'I figure we should square up, tell him we want our share, then clear this neck of the woods.'

Bowdrie had been glaring at him as they started working the horses through the mesquite. 'Ralls wouldn't hold out on us! Not after all we've done together.'

Bodine snorted. 'You figure Ralls would show *us* any loyalty? Hell, man, way I see it, we're gonna be chasin' our tails while Ralls is livin' it up in Mexico City!'

'And if that's right, you'd still be stupid enough to tackle him and ask for a split?'

'Hell, we've earned it!'

'We-ell, that's as maybe, but Zack always said you can't out-smart Ralls. He plays the cards his way. Stir him up and he'll kill you before you can say your own name.'

Bigelow declined to argue, seemed sorry he had even raised the subject now. Bowdrie, looking thoughtful, said: 'Well, mebbe it is time we caught up with Ralls. We been workin' for weeks, done all the chores so far. We'll remind him we're still around – and you can drop a hint about divvyin'-up the loot.' He added a thin smile. 'I'll wait and see how Ralls takes it before I put in my two cents' worth!'

'It better be a helluva lot more'n that!'

Bigelow wrenched his mount's head around, fighting the animal, pulling out a handful of mane. The horse tried to bite his leg and he almost fell. Bowdrie laughed.

'Let's go find our saddles and bridles before you do yourself an injury.'

'I ain't the one gotta worry about injuries! By the time I'm finished, that damned Silent'll wish he'd let the wolves tear him apart!'

'Those two won't be at all happy with you,' remarked Gail as she and Silent sat their horses within a screen of brush up on the rimrock, watching the antics of the men below. 'Bigelow's having a lot of trouble staying on.'

'Long as he lands on his head he won't get hurt.'

She glanced at him sharply. 'You have a strange sense of humour. I'm not sure if you mean it as a joke, or are really being callous.'

He said nothing, gaze following the struggling men below as they made their way back towards the cave where they had recently held Silent prisoner. The girl unsheathed her rifle in a smooth, slick movement that caught Silent off-guard. But he snapped to attention when she swiftly worked the lever.

The foresight and the end of the barrel moved in a slow arc as she tracked one of the men below.

'If he was a turkey, I could shoot Bigelow's left eye clean out from here,' she said.

Silent had been about to admonish her, changed his mind about what he was going to say, folded his hands on his saddle horn. 'Do it,' he rapped.

She stiffened, her eyes flicking towards him, but she looked down the barrel again quickly.

'What're you waiting for? He'll be behind those rocks in a few seconds! Blow him out of the saddle!'

Her body stiffened even more as she still

held her pose. He could hear her breathing – fast, not slow and easy like someone steadying to make sure of the target.

'You can relax now. He's gone.'

Her face was pale and tight as she looked towards him, lowering the rifle's hammer. She dropped her gaze.

'Damn you! Why do you make me feel so – foolish?'

'Just seeing if you realize shooting a man ain't as easy as shooting clay or paper targets.'

Her lips were tight against her teeth, eyes blazing. 'D'you think I don't know that! I can shoot the pip out of an ace of spades at forty paces, or blow a dime to glory, firing off-hand at a hundred yards – but I'm not able to blow a man out of the saddle – at something like sixty yards! You just saw for yourself! Happy now?'

'You *could* do it. If you really wanted to.'

Her nostrils flared. She was silent for a time, breathing deeply with emotion. Both men below had disappeared into the cave area now and she sheathed the Winchester. Then she said, sharply, 'You don't believe I can!'

He shrugged. 'I believe you're as fine a shot as you claim.'

'But you don't think I'm capable of killing someone?'

'Not yet.'

'What does that mean?'

'Reckon you'll work up to it.'

'You're an expert in what people will or won't do, are you?'

He shook his head. 'One or both of them two killed your father. You'll do it when you have to.'

'Yes – I will.' She was quiet for a long time before she said in a smaller voice without the edge of anger, 'Unless you beat me to it.'

He smiled. 'There's that.'

'You – have no compunction about killing?'

'Depends.'

'On what?'

He touched his bandanna and loosened it a little. 'Throats getting sore again.'

'How convenient!'

He didn't comment on that and turned his horse, dropping off the rim and on to the outside slope of the draw. She didn't follow right away, sat her mount, a sleek claybank, watching, and saw where he was heading.

Gail nodded to herself.

Aggravating or not, he knew what he was about: he was making for the only exit

Bigelow and Bowdrie could take to clear that end of the draw.

Still a little mad at him, she set the claybank down the slope in his tracks.

He paused and she was almost up level with him when he shouted as loud as he was capable of and lifted his reins.

'*Get off the rim!*' It was a rasping garble, the last word drowned by the crashing of more than one rifle. Then rock chips were buzzing, stinging the legs of their horses. She had good reactions and wrenched her reins, sliding the claybank down below the rim so she was no longer a target against the sky.

Silent was crouched low on his horse, rifle in hand, weaving the roan through the brush, turning his head slightly to call something to her. Gail couldn't make out the words, but she figured it was some kind of warning, and when she saw his rifle barrel angle across his lap and point downwards, she turned the claybank down the slope.

The hidden guns spoke again, lead raking the shale and rattling the brush as they forced a way through. Her heart was hammering as she followed Silent, figuring this was more his kind of deal than hers. He was dropping lower down the slope all the time and she briefly wondered about this.

Wouldn't he be leaving the shooters above him? On the high ground? Giving them the advantage?

Suddenly, he disappeared – man and horse.

One second Silent was spurring across the slope, next he was gone. Gail instinctively started to haul rein, fearing that he had ridden clean off the edge of a drop before he was able to stop. Her heart came up into her throat as she realized this was exactly what had happened – though later she learned he had deliberately ridden over the short drop down into a small, saucer-shaped clearing, edged with some brush and a few dozen scattered rocks.

She cried out as the wind whistled past her face and knocked her hat off, so that it hung and twisted down her back on the rawhide tie-thong. Then the claybank's legs jarred on the loose earth of the slope and she had her hands full trying to keep the horse on an even keel. The claybank shrilled but apparently was used to this type of country. *One advantage of hiring locally…*

Silent swung his roan in against the claybank from the downslope side, steadying it, and in seconds she was in full control. He veered away, throwing a leg over the saddle horn and quitting leather with his rifle. He dropped to the loose earth, slid, rolled a few yards and squirmed behind a clump of rocks.

She figured she could do worse than follow his lead and, breathless, body jarred, she settled a couple of yards from him. She started to speak but his rifle triggered in three fast, raking shots. Glancing up in the direction the barrel was angled, she saw dust spurt at the base of some brush and was about to look away when a man lurched upright. He staggered, clawing at his chest or upper arm – dust and powder smoke blurring the image – and then he tumbled forward, flopped a few yards and lay still. Brush moved up there again and Silent instantly fired. She heard a muted curse. The bushes jerked more. A rifle barrel appeared and a series of shots probed the rocks where they lay. Silent fired again and an arm appeared between two rocks, hanging limply.

Gail hunkered down, gave a startled cry as a rock chip stung the back of her left hand and she shook it involuntarily. She glimpsed a man's shirt between rocks, just a small flash of colour, threw the rifle to her shoulder without conscious effort, beaded and fired.

Rockdust erupted and the shirt disappeared. Gail felt the blood drain from her face and a shocked voice shouted in her mind, *Oh my God! I think I just shot a man!*

Silent had moved, rolling rather than getting his knees under him. He gestured angrily to her to get down low just as a bullet whipped air past her face. She dropped swiftly, gasping, trembling hands feeling the hot breech of the rifle, automatically working the lever. She swallowed as she raised the weapon and this time deliberately looked for a target above. In the end she just fired a short burst.

She pressed her face into the earth as bullets raked her cover. Silent's rifle crackled in a brief volley and, seconds later, she glimpsed running men up there, diving over the ridge, lead snarling around them. A man staggered, righted and stumbled on. Silent vaulted up and began running, crouched almost double, over to the left. She saw that this was the edge of the saucer and there seemed nothing but space beyond.

He dropped on to his belly right at the very rim, threw the smoking rifle to his shoulder and got off two shots before the hammer fell on an empty breech. He spun on to his back and began to shuck cartridges from his belt and push them through the rifle's loading gate.

He didn't seem to be in any hurry and she moved slowly across, crouching below him slightly. 'Have they gone?'

'Going. They'll be outta sight before I'm reloaded. Hurry 'em along!'

But she didn't shoot. 'How – how many were there?'

'Four – mebbe five. Plus Bigelow and Bowdrie.'

She glanced at the slope where the man that Silent had shot still lay, unmoving. And she could see the shirt of the one she had aimed at through the brush now – also unmoving – the cloth stained with blood.

'I – I think I shot one.'

'Yeah. We'll go talk with him.'

'Is he – still alive?' She couldn't keep the elation and relief from her voice.

'Could be.'

'What about that man on the slope you shot?'

'He's dead.'

'How can you be sure?'

'I shot to kill. Might've got another, too. Know I winged one more.' He led the way across the slope and she went with reluctance and trepidation but felt a flood of relief when Silent stepped forward quickly and kicked a six-gun out of reach of the groping hand of the man lying on the ground. There was a good deal of blood on the checked shirt and her relief faded swiftly as the owner turned a grey, gaunted face towards her, silently accusing.

'Know him?'

Startled at Silent's question, she barely glanced at the stubbled, pain-contorted face and shook her head quickly.

'Think I saw him in St David. That right, *amigo?*'

'Go to – hell!' the wounded man gritted.

Silent nodded slowly. 'So that's how you want it.' He took a deep breath, rasping, 'Gail, you might like to get the horses and tie them to that tree with the crooked trunk – down there.'

He pointed ten yards downslope and she gave him a sharp look. He stared back. 'So I won't see … anything?'

'You might still hear. Just don't look up.'

Her face was a mixture of abhorrence and anger as she tried to find the right words. But Silent looked almost amused as he slanted his gaze towards the wounded man.

'Wha – what you gonna do to me?' the man asked hoarsely.

'Up to you. Only want answers to a few questions. How you do it...' Silent spread his hands and shrugged.

Then he took out his hunting-knife. The wounded man grunted, tried to back away but he was losing too much blood and there was a lot of pain. The girl moved downslope now, her pace increasing as she spotted the mounts and went after them. She resisted the urge to look back.

Silent leaned over the man, knife blade placed under the stubbled chin. The bushwhacker shrank back, eyes bulging.

'That shotgun guard was my kid brother.'

'Aw, God! I – think I'm gonna be sick!'

'Just keep it off my boots.'

Silent put some pressure on the blade, felt the point prick the man's skin. A terrified scream raked the slope with rising terror...

Gail jumped, standing just within the trees, hands shaking as she held the reins of both horses, staring, white-faced, to where Silent's stooped body hid whatever he was doing to the wounded man.

Hurriedly, trembling, she tied the reins to the tree and started back up the slope, stumbling in her hurry, clinging to her rifle. 'Stop! *Stop* that at once!'

'Stay down there!' Silent half-shouted

without turning. 'You won't like this!'

And the wounded man began to scream in wild terror.

She didn't really want to see – but she couldn't just let him continue torturing that man – a man she had shot...

Slowly, Silent straightened, his hands bloody. He turned and looked at her standing a few yards below him, strongly disapproving. 'He's passed out.'

Breathing hard, deliberately swinging her rifle towards him now, she made herself take a few steps closer.

'My God, I – I don't know why I don't shoot you! How could I stand by and let you – do whatever you did to that man who was already suffering?'

Silent held out one bloody hand and she saw a shapeless lump of something in the palm. Her eyes raised to his face, puzzled. 'What's that?'

'Your bullet.' She sucked in a sharp breath. 'Busted one of his ribs, lodged under the skin, pressing on another.'

She was frowning. 'I – don't understand. You removed the bullet?'

He nodded. 'That's all.'

Her mouth opened to speak but no words came for a moment. Then, 'And you – let him believe you were...!'

'He just used his imagination. Likely had watched Bowdrie working on Larry, figured he was in for the same.' Gail sat down on the slope, nursing the rifle across her thighs now. She shook her head, flaxen hair swinging. 'I – I didn't know what I was getting into when I decided to look for the men who killed my father! With *you* for company!'

'We'll find them. Unless you want to go back?'

'No! Damn you. I – I *can't* quit! I won't!'

'I savvy that. Was wondering if you did.'

'I don't know if I can take all – this. Dammit, I'm a *dressmaker*, who enjoys a little target shooting as a hobby. I – have to admit, I'm out of my depth here.'

He glanced at the unconscious man and sat down beside her, toying with the mis-shapen bullet. 'Get some cloth to bind his wound. He's still bleeding plenty.'

She fetched rags from her saddlebags and they bound the wound firmly. With plenty of pauses, Silent spoke.

Between screams of terror, believing he was going to be flayed alive like young Larry Clay, the wounded man, who claimed his name was 'Blackie' White, sobbed out in-formation.

His companions who had tried to ambush Silent and Gail were led by a man named Ralls. He was in on the planning for the theft of the gold – which they knew Ralls had hidden somewhere. Shorty Creed, the wounded man Doc Jones had taken to Bisbee for medical treatment, had sent a wire to Ralls, telling him about Silent heading for the draw where the stage was wrecked. *Gratitude, real gratitude.*

Silent worried them: they hadn't realized he was so deadly. And they reckoned to get rid of him before he killed them all. Blackie confirmed it was Zack and Will Bowdrie and Bodine who had worked on Larry, not realizing – or caring – the kid was a greenhorn.

'Why'd they give him the job?' Silent rasped.

'Needed to make it look like the stage carried somethin' worth guardin'. Kid was so eager, he woulda done the job for no pay.'

'Decoy?'

Blackie nodded, sobbing his words by now. 'We – dressed like Injuns – hit the stage – there was no gold, of course – Ralls had already hid it, but rigged the stage attack just the same so folk'd think that was when the gold was stolen.'

'And you had to butcher everyone to make it look like they'd been tortured for the same reason.'

'We din' know for sure it wasn't there!' Blackie squirmed as Silent's blade moved threateningly. 'Was the Bowdries started the really rough stuff.'

'You were there.'

'No! Zack an' Will took the kid an' that young gal into the brush – did their devil's work. We – we heard screamin'...'

Silent stopped speaking. The girl looked at him. She was pale, her face taut. 'This must be – awful for you.'

'Has to be done.'

And she knew he *would* do whatever it took, to find the men who had killed his brother.

As she had suspected earlier, the gold didn't mean a damn thing to him.

'Now what?' She gestured to Blackie who was moaning softly, a hand holding his side.

'Take him with us to St David, I guess. I need to talk with Sheriff Lyall. And that stageline agent.'

She smiled faintly to herself. 'Oh. That's the reason. Not to see the man gets proper medical treatment?'

His eyes made her flinch. 'I don't care

about that. Only if it'll make him tell me more.'

Feeling a sudden chill in her chest, she knew he wasn't joking.

He was as ruthless and merciless as the men he hunted – and he intended to kill them all, one by one.

CHAPTER 8

BACKTRAIL

Sheriff Lyall came into his office, turned to lock the passage door after him. Gail frowned, glanced at Silent who remained impassive.

'That man really needs medical attention, Sheriff,' Gail said sharply. 'It's why we brought him in.'

He dropped the keys on the battered desk with a clatter, sat down in his chair, moved his buttocks to a more comfortable position and folded his big hands in his lap. Only then did he deign to look at the girl. 'You patched him up pretty good. If I think he needs a sawbones, he'll get one.'

'But – a jail cell is not the best place for a wounded man, surely? He's still losing blood.'

'Better'n being left out in the wilds.' Lyall flicked his gaze to Silent. 'Calls himself "Blackie White", but his real name's Whitford. There's a dodger or two on him. Armed robbery, assault.' The chill gaze returned to the girl. 'His welfare isn't a priority with me, ma'am.' Gail's mouth tightened. 'Perhaps it would've been better if we'd gone all the way back to Bisbee with him.' Lyall shrugged, uninterested, set his gaze on Silent. 'You've had time enough to think about your own name by now, mister.'

'Still like "Silent".'

'I don't. You remembered? Or do I have to nudge you along?'

'Yeah, do that, Sheriff.' Silent glanced at the girl although he spoke to the lawman.

Lyall almost smiled and turned to Gail Cobb. 'You know he's a good cook?'

'I heard he was a popular trail cook, yes.'

'Uh-huh. Where you learn to cook so well, mister?'

'Chef from one of the big hotels in San Francisco showed me how.'

'Well, he'd be a good man for the job. Where you meet someone like that? I mean, a drifter like you?'

'We worked together in a kitchen. He saw I was interested, took me under his wing.'

'This kitchen – where?'

Silent gave the lawman an expressionless stare but Gail was sure there was some anger burning way back in his eyes. 'I reckon you're dyin' to tell Gail yourself. So why don't you?'

Lyall grunted, face unfriendly as he took his time looking at the girl. 'Yuma Penitentiary. He had two years to learn. Seems his time wasn't altogether wasted.'

Gail's face reflected her surprise. She frowned.

Lyall went on speaking: 'Two years for killing a man in Prescott. Not much of a sentence for taking a man's life but the judge decided it was a fair gunfight, and the dead man had terrorized the south-west for a long time, anyways. He was glad to get rid of him, I dare say. So he went soft on Silent here – or "Aaron Clay", as he was called at that time. But figured it wouldn't hurt to get him off the streets. And Yuma could always use another man on the rockpile.'

'So – you're a real gunfighter?'

A small smile tugged at one corner of his mouth. 'Dunno any unreal ones, ma'am.'

She made an impatient sign with her hand. 'Oh, you know what I mean! You have a – reputation as a fast gun.'

He said nothing. Lyall seemed as if he wanted to elaborate on that but apparently changed his mind. 'Can't find a dodger on you now with any apprehension orders still outstanding, so guess you must've served all your time, Clay.'

'I served enough.'

'Now that sounds almost like a challenge. You kinda hinting there *might* still be a dodger I dunno about?'

'How would you expect me to answer that?'

Lyall sat up, rolled a cigarette, and while he lit up, tossed the sack and papers to Silent, who shook his head.

'Smoking makes my throat too dry. But thanks, anyway, Sheriff.'

'Time you told me what you're really doing in my bailiwick, Clay.'

Silent rubbed his throat slowly before answering. 'After the men who killed my brother, ridin' shotgun on the Tombstone stage.'

Lyall's eyebrows arched. 'That kid? The one they ... butchered?' He let his words drift off. 'Well, it sounds gospel, what you say. But you know how I feel about someone coming into my county and taking the law into their own hands?'

Silent shook his head, and Lyall straightened in the chair. 'I've been attacked and I defended myself, Sheriff. That's all. You can't jail a man for that.'

Lyall's eyes narrowed. 'Yeah. You've been around. You've had plenty of these conversations, I'll bet. But – I've told you, Clay. Now you know – and if you step on my toes, you also know what to expect.' He stood abruptly, nodding to Gail. 'I guess you're eager to get washed-up, ma'am. I can recommend the *Bijou* boarding house. Clean, reasonable rates. Ladies only.'

'Thank you, Sheriff.' Her tone was neutral.

'You won't be staying long, I expect.' The lawman addressed these words to Silent, who shrugged.

'Got a couple calls to make.'

Lyall glanced out the window. 'Be through by sundown.'

Silent held the door for Gail and she hesitated briefly, then stepped outside into the afternoon sunlight. He closed the door behind him, his body brushing hers on the small porch. 'The sheriff seems very ... touchy about his jurisdiction.'

'Got this town tamed way down and wants to keep it that way, I reckon. I dunno if he's as tough as he makes out but he likes to get his way.'

'He doesn't sound all that interested in what happened to the stage.'

'Was weeks ago and only just overlaps his

territory.' He said that off the top of his head, but the girl's words made him think a mite deeper about Lyall and his apparent indifference to the stage robbery; a man as jealous of his reputation as the sheriff surely would want to get to the bottom of the massacre – and collect any kudos that came his way?

The stageline clerk didn't seem any less languid than when Silent had seen him before, until he recognized the man standing on the opposite side of the scarred, paper-strewn desk.

Then he straightened abruptly and the dead match he was chewing on slid out of the corner of his slack mouth and fell unnoticed to the floor. Silent kept staring and the man swallowed, nodding briefly.

'Oh – howdy! Didn't recognize you against the light. Thought you'd left town.'

'Who hired the shotgun guard?' Silent asked without preamble.

The agent blinked. 'Er ... that'd be the guard on the special Tombstone run?'

'You know who I'm talking about.'

The man scratched his ear. 'Well ... think I told you, all arrangements were made through Head Office.'

'That kid wasn't in Tucson when he was

hired.' Silent was guessing but, knowing Larry, it seemed logical to him and the clerk began shuffling papers nervously, revealing a narrow, desktop name-board lying amongst them as he gathered them into a pile. The name on the board was Chapman Ralls...

Silent remembered then: when Blackie had told him the leader of the bushwhackers was named 'Ralls' he knew he had heard or seen the name before. It must have been on his earlier visit to this office, on this name-board.

Silent pointed to the slim piece of varnished wood. 'What do they call you? "Chap"? "Chappie"? Or just "Ralls"?'

The man shook his head. 'That's the agent, my boss. He's over Bisbee, Contention way. My name's Link Roper. I'm just the booking clerk.'

'Ralls travel around much?'

'Sure. He's Head Agent in this part of the territory. Has to checkout the depots regularly.'

'Does he ever go to Tucson?'

'Now and again, when he has to make a report about somethin' important, or company policy is gonna change.' His smile broadened. 'Which usually means the fares are goin' up.'

'How about Huachuca City?'

'Well ... mebbe. He's interested in some old mines down that way. More personal than for the company, which, incidentally, owns this stageline.'

That was news to Silent. 'Mebbe he hired the guard?'

'Well ... now you mention it, mebbe he did. He did say there'd be a greenhorn ridin' shotgun on the Tombstone run. Nothin' much important bein' carried but it'd give him some experience. I dunno as he actually *hired* the kid, though.'

'When d'you expect Ralls back here?'

Roper spread his hands. 'Who knows? He's his own boss, can wander all over the territory if he wants before comin' back to St David.'

'Thanks, Link. You've been a big help.'

'Din' mean to be – I mean – din' realize it!' Sweat broke out on the man's gawky face and Silent smiled thinly.

'Better mop your face. Sweat can sting your eyes pretty bad – your mouth, too.'

Reaching for a kerchief, Link Roper stopped, frowning. 'My mouth? Never stung my mouth – just tastes salty.'

'You never know. Best to make sure, keep your mouth shut. Savvy?'

Silent left and Roper blinked, watching him through the doorway as he crossed the street. Then he wiped his damp face with a shaky hand.

That feller with the hoarse voice was one scary *hombre*. He didn't even have to work at it – one look into those piercing dark eyes and your heart rate went through the roof, while the bottom dropped out of your belly.

Link decided it was time for some sort of bracer. He went to a cupboard and arranged the door part-way open so that anyone entering couldn't see what he was doing. Then he reached into the back, behind an untidy stack of files, and brought out a flat bottle with a crudely printed label that read 'Genuwyne Kentucky Burbon'.

He drank a good draught, coughed and gasped.

'Closest this slop has been to Kentucky is Yargo's moonshine still in the brush behind the saloon.'

But it hit the spot. To make sure, he took another swig.

Tate Scorsby, the livery man, nodded in friendly manner when Silent walked down the aisle towards where he was working at repairing a loose slat in a stall partition. He straightened, holding a hammer down at his side, some nails protruding between the fingers of his other hand.

'Back again? I hear with nice-lookin' company this time. Least, the one ridin' upright was.'

Silent nodded. 'The other one on the spare horse was Blackie White – or Whitford. Know him?'

The livery man's face was sober now. 'Not "know". But he raises hell most times he hits town. Which ain't too often now Lyall's sheriff.'

'When was he here last?'

'Aw ... mebbe a couple months. No. Not as long as that. Make it six weeks ago.'

'Just before the trouble with the stage?'

Tate was wary now. 'He hired three hosses. I never got 'em back.'

'Three?'

'One for himself. One for his sidekick – another hardcase. Other for the kid.'

Silent tensed. 'What kid?'

'The one rode shotgun on the stage. The one they chopped up.'

'His name was Larry Clay. My brother.'

Tate stepped back. 'Well, pardon me all to hell, mister, I din' mean to talk so – straight. If I'd knowed he was kin...'

Silent held up a hand. 'They say where they were going?'

'Up to Benson, to pick up the stage down to Tombstone, I believe they said. That's why I never worried too much about the hosses not coming back. Knew Ralls'd see me right. He runs a good stageline, a fair man. Tough, and hard as petrified wood, but mostly fair.'

'Sure it was Benson and not Huachuca?' The man shrugged uncertainly. Silent asked, 'Why would Ralls hire two hardcases like Blackie and his sidekick?'

Tate shrugged. 'They was goin' that way anyhow an' he wanted the kid to have some protection.' He looked away and added in a low voice, 'He sure was green, you don't mind me sayin' so.'

'Yeah. He'd've been way out of his depth. Could've got lost real easy.'

Silent eased his six-gun holster to a more comfortable position on his hip, seeing the livery man tense. He smiled faintly. 'Got time for a beer?'

Scorsby looked regretful. 'Not right now, sorry to say. Mebbe later?'

'Might be leaving soon. But next time I see you in the saloon.' Silent casually touched a finger to his hatbrim and walked out of the stables.

He found Gail Cobb in a café near the *Bijou* Ladies Boarding House. She was smartened up some since her bath and sponging and ironing her clothes. She looked up in surprise as he pulled out a chair across the small table from her.

'Howdy. You smell nice.'

She smiled, lowered her gaze as he ordered a coffee and sandwich from the waitress. She watched his face. 'What's happened?'

'Nothing much. But you said you saw Larry in Bisbee. When was that?'

Small lines appeared between her eyes as she thought.

'About six weeks ago.'

Silent nodded. 'He wasn't supposed to be there. He should've been in Benson, waiting to pick up the stage when it came across from Tucson. I think he'd been given that Bisbee run just for "training", so it'd look better when the stage was held up.'

'That's awful! It would mean they deliberately set him up to – to be killed!'

'That's what they did.' His voice was flat, hard and cold, almost free of the rasping edge.

She toyed with her coffee cup while the waitress brought Silent's coffee and sandwich. He took a bite and spoke around the food. 'Why was he was in Bisbee at all?'

She didn't answer because she didn't know. Then as he tapped fingers of his free hand on the table and took another bite of his sandwich, she asked, 'Why is Bisbee so important?'

He swallowed again, wincing once more, took a big sip of coffee. 'I think maybe there wasn't any gold on that stage when it finally left Bisbee.'

'Well, they kept saying there was nothing of value in the express box, but that only convinced most folk there was.'

'Which was what they wanted folk to think. But there was no gold carried on that stage. It may've appeared on the lading bills under some other name but they had Larry deliver it to Bisbee first. They'd've told him the run was just for him to get "experience", I reckon.'

Her mouth dropped open briefly. 'You mean the attack on the stage was to cover up the fact that the gold had already been stolen?' Aghast, she shook her head quickly. 'There was no gold on board when the stage reached the draw – and the raiders knew it! Which means all those people: my father, Larry, the passengers – died for nothing!'

'Just to convince folk – or someone in particular, maybe – that the gold that was *supposed* to be on the stage was stolen by the renegades.'

'What do you mean – "someone in particular"?'

'Just a wild notion. Someone high up had to be in on it. We better go see Blackie Whitford again.'

When they reached the law office it was empty and the door leading to the cellblock passage stood halfway open. There was a heavy silence that even seemed to shut out the street sounds.

Both of them felt it, exchanged glances, the girl tensing. Silent drew his pistol, motioned for her to wait there, but she followed him into the shadowed passage.

At the far end the door of the cell allotted to Blackie Whitford stood open. It was prevented from closing by a man lying face down on the floor, half-in and half-out of the cell. Gail gasped and Silent motioned emphatically for her to stay back. There was no sign of Blackie.

He knelt quickly by the body, recognizing Sheriff Lyall, blood matting the usually neatly combed grey-shot hair at the back of his head. His Colt was still in the holster which told Silent, even as he reached to check for a pulse in the lawman's neck, that Lyall hadn't been suspicious of his attacker. *Or had reacted too slowly.*

Silent found a pulse, slow but steady and strong enough. Quite a lot of blood was on the bunk and the floor of the cell.

'Is he – dead?'

Silent shook his head, standing slowly. 'Better fetch the sawbones. He's had one helluva belt on the head.'

He stood there as she hurried out, holstering his gun now, trying to read the sign of the bloodstained blankets trailing over the edge of the bunk, the smeared blood on the stone floor, even on the barred door.

Looked to him like Blackie Whitford had somehow busted his wound open – or had *had* it busted open when he was forcibly dragged from the cell.

Either way, he was missing, and Silent was more convinced than ever now that the man knew more than he had let on.

A lot more.

Enough, maybe, to get him killed.

CHAPTER 9

DEATH TRAIL

Lyall's eyes were still a trifle glazed but there was a hard resentment in them as he looked at Silent, Gail and the doctor from under the swathe of bandages on his head. He lifted his gaze to the medico's pale, taut features.

'How come you got involved in this, Doc?'

The man was nervous, his long-fingered bony hands trembling. 'Sheriff – I – I had to do what they wanted! They left a man with my wife! She – she's absolutely distraught still, at her – experience, and I'd appreciate it if you could let me return to her as soon as possible.'

'How come you were involved?' Lyall repeated doggedly and more loudly.

'I told you. Two men came into my infirmary, one claiming to have stomach pains. It was all a fake, of course. Once inside, he put a gun to my wife's head, said if I took the other man to see the prisoner, she would be released unharmed and...'

It was easily accomplished, of course, although Lyall wanted to know how the men knew he was holding the prisoner who, they claimed, was a friend of theirs.

Lyall interrupted the doctor's halting explanations – he really didn't know anything and was guessing wildly – and looked at Silent. 'I was a mite suspicious, but I've known Doc Kettle here for twenty years. I *didn't* know the varmint who was with him, but if he said he was a friend of Blackie Whitmore's, he was no friend of mine.'

'Your Colt was still in your holster when we found you.'

Lyall's mouth tightened bitterly. 'Like I said, I trusted Doc Kettle. Got careless. Let the other son of a bitch get behind me and ... well, what did happen, Doc?'

The medic was wringing his hands by this time, obviously worried about his wife. 'The man hit you with his gun butt, shoved me out into the passage and told me to go home and tell his friend all was OK. I didn't waste any time but I did see him dragging the prisoner out of his bunk by his arm. I knew the man's wound would break open and – I'm sorry, Sheriff – I was most concerned about Esther – as I am now, and...'

The lawman lifted a hand, then swiftly grasped the chair arm. 'OK, Doc. Go on home and tend to Esther. It's not your fault.'

The sawbones started to turn, swung back. 'Sheriff, you'll need to rest. That was a severe blow and you'll suffer a reaction very soon, I think. I'll come back and give you something – but you need to rest right now. And I mean *rest!*'

Lyall glared but he looked grey and Silent noticed his hands were gripping the arms of his chair hard enough to whiten the gnarled knuckles. He was hurt more than he allowed to show.

When the medic had gone, Lyall squinted at Silent and the girl. 'Got an opinion?'

'It seems to me,' Gail said before Silent could speak, 'that the prisoner was important to the two men who arranged his escape. But – all that blood!'

'Yes. They were rough. Clay?'

'They didn't want Blackie in jail. Mebbe afraid he'd tell something they didn't want him to.'

'If they just wanted to shut his mouth, they could've shot him through the window – or even after they jumped me.'

'Mebbe they wanted to check first – see how much he'd already told us.'

The sheriff nodded in slow agreement and Silent said, 'They're burning the miles from here by the minute, Sheriff.'

'Ever been a deputy? Aw, don't look so surprised. I guess it was a stupid question to ask someone like you, anyway. But I need someone official trailing those fugitives until I can ride again.' His eyes squinted, obviously pain was reaching him now and he swayed in the chair. 'I need live prisoners, not a trail of dead men. I'll deputize you and you'll be bound by the law–'

'Not me.' Silent spoke firmly, his words unmistakably clear. He stood and began to move towards the door.

'Come back here, dammit!' Lyall started to rise from the chair but collapsed back into it, breathing hard, dizzy.

Gail caught up with Silent as he was striding towards the livery. She grabbed his arm but he kept going and she had to almost jog to keep up. 'Aren't you being foolish?'

'I don't see it.'

'But if you had an official law badge...?'

He paused, slapped a hand against his Colt. 'This is all I need.'

She stopped then, but he kept moving.

After a few moments, when he dodged

through the traffic towards the livery, she made her decision and hurried after him.

Gail reined in her claybank on the high ledge and watched Silent dismount from the roan and check the ground once more for tracks. She admitted to herself that he was much better at this than she was; she could track a turkey or a rabbit, but man-tracking was beyond her talents. So she had followed him out of town, at a distance, trying not to make her presence known – but she suspected he knew anyway.

In point of fact, she didn't really know why she was following him. She knew what would happen if – when – he caught up with the two men and Blackie Whitmore. But she had a strange feeling of – responsibility.

She felt she had to do what she could to ensure Blackie's welfare. Arguing with herself, she knew Silent would consider it strange – stupid, even – but she *had* wounded Blackie in the first place; was actually pleased the man was still alive when they brought him to St David.

She shuddered slightly, recalling all that blood in the cell. The wound must be busted wide open, and she knew Blackie wouldn't last long, bleeding like that. She also knew the men who had snatched him from the jail would not pause to bandage the wound or give it attention in any way. Except, maybe in one way, which she tried not to think about.

She was more than a little afraid they would kill Blackie, to make sure he didn't talk about them, and although it was probably foolish, she already suspected she would feel responsible for his death.

Her other fear was that Silent would go in alone, gun blazing in a storm of bullets.

Suddenly, bringing her mind back to the present with a thud, she realized something was wrong.

Silent was gone.

She couldn't see him anywhere. 'That's not possible!' she murmured, standing in the stirrups, searching slowly. 'He can't have disappeared into thin air.'

But there was no sign of him. Frowning, she looked again at where he had dismounted and examined the ground. She swallowed as she noticed for the first time the large dark stain on the earth at the edge of stubble grass where he had searched for sign.

It could be blood, drag-marks of blood.

A few feet beyond the grass, she saw that there was a sudden drop: the perspective had at first masked it, making it appear as one long, undulating slope of stubble grass. Now, from this angle, she could discern the line where there was a gap, the edge of some kind of ditch.

Heart hammering, she set the claybank down from the ledge, hurriedly sliding the rifle out from the saddle case under her right leg. She didn't dismount when she reached the place where she had last seen Silent, merely leaned forward, looking down. Yes! She could make out traces of horseshoes where they had bent the stiff grass and it hadn't yet sprung back all the way. Her pulse raced wildly as she realized that this meant the tracks had been made not too long ago. But she edged the horse towards the gap in the slope. It appeared to widen as she approached. The horse didn't want to get too close and she tightened the rein, half-stood and leaned over the claybank's head. The buzzing of flies made her catch her breath.

Blackie Whitford lay in the bottom of the ditch, bloody and dirt-caked. There was a bullet hole in his head. Gail looked away swiftly. Those wide, staring glazed eyes seeming to follow her movements.

She felt her stomach churn. 'I – I'm not

cut out for this!' she murmured. But a flash of her father's face brought her up straighter in the saddle and she saw how it really was, how Silent had tried to tell her. This man in the ditch had no doubt been part of the gang who had caused her father's death. And she was here to avenge him. But she didn't seem to have the wherewithal to kill another human being. Yet, how could she condemn Silent for doing exactly what she *wanted* to do but seemed incapable of? The thing was, he could handle it: she couldn't.

'I could've shot you seven ways to Sunday.'

She twisted in the saddle at the sound of the hoarse voice behind her. He was half-screened by brush, afoot, holding his rifle across his chest.

'Couldn't see clearly in the brush. Nearly fired.'

She swallowed, making herself look calm, though she felt far from that. 'Did you... finish Blackie?'

He shook his head. 'Reckon he'd lost so much blood he was likely dead before they put one in him to make sure.'

'How ... how can you be so casual about it?' He didn't answer. Then she licked her dry lips and said, 'D'you know who we're following?'

'"We"? OK, leave that. The two who took him from jail, of course, but I don't know their names.'

'Where are they?' She couldn't help looking around.

'Likely watching us from the rim. No! Don't raise your head. Let 'em think we're too busy arguing to worry about them.'

'But ... my God! They could shoot us!'

'Uh-huh.'

'Well ... hadn't we better get under cover?'

'Good idea,' he agreed but she had the notion he was silently laughing at her.

Her mouth tightened. 'Where?'

'Down in the ditch with Blackie'd be the best place.'

'Wha–? What're you saying? I can't climb down there with – that! It'd be like – crawling into a grave.'

Then there was a rifle shot and he lunged at her, knocking her out of the saddle, letting her horse run; it was smart enough to find cover. He kept his hold on her as they both rolled into the ditch. The girl scrambled frantically to keep clear of Blackie Whitford's corpse. Silent dropped on to the inward slope of the ditch and his rifle blasted two shots as more lead chewed grass and dirt from the edge of the ditch. She

124

cringed as this was flung over her hat and shoulders, put down a hand, and withdrew it quickly with a sharp intake of breath as she felt sticky blood.

'Start shooting! Make 'em keep their heads down.'

His rifle was hammering, but not in wild, rapid-fire volleys. His shots were paced, and she knew he must have targets. Wiping her bloody hand on the grass, she got the rifle butt into her shoulder, glimpsed a man's hat up on the rim and took swift aim.

She fired and the hat spun away, Gail sucking in a quick breath. *My God! Did she hit the hat's owner...?*

Then she heard a sound off to her left and below her. Half-rolling she looked across Silent's prone body and, to her horror, saw a man rising from a rock at the far end of the ditch, bringing a rifle to his shoulder.

Gail reacted instinctively: the man was obviously going to murder Silent who had no idea the killer was even there, concentrating as he was on the rim. There was no time for a warning: she just lifted her rifle and triggered, a single shot.

It was enough. The bullet passed over Silent's prone body and the man at the end of the ditch seemed to jump into the air, his body hurled backwards, head snapping back as if it would fly off his shoulders. He was still falling awkwardly when Silent spun on to his side, saw the killer sprawling and swiftly figured what had happened.

He glanced at her – not without some surprise – and nodded his thanks. Then he turned back to the rim and fired four shots. She saw the spray of rocks and gravel, thought she heard a shouted curse of surprise, although her ears were ringing wildly with the echoing gunfire. There was movement up there and, as Silent hurriedly reloaded, he yelled while thumbing home cartridges: 'Stop him!'

When he saw she had frozen, he stifled a curse and slammed three shots at the rim. Swearing, he thrust to his feet, ran up out of the ditch and caught the reins of her claybank as it started out of the brush. He swung lithely into the saddle and, holding the rifle out to one side, the reins in his left hand, raked his bootheels into the mount's flanks.

Panicked a little, Gail clambered up out of the ditch-grave, calling to him. But Silent was racing along the ledge, swinging out of sight behind a massive grey egg of granite.

Panting, she ran to the rock and watched

as he urged the claybank up the steep trail. Above, she saw a man on a chestnut pause on the rim, triggering two shots down at his pursuer. He wheeled his mount, spurred away along the rim with Silent urging the claybank up on to the flat.

She lost sight of both men then.

Silent's quarry weaved and zigzagged his chestnut through the huge rocks jutting out of the harsh landscape. It was obvious that he knew this country pretty well, as he rounded a clump of boulders and apparently disappearing.

Silent hauled rein, then saw the dust haze swirling between two broken slabs, just wide enough for horse and rider. The fugitive had gone through full tilt but Silent had to slow down and work the claybank through. He was halfway when the killer opened up from beyond, ricocheting his bullets from one wall to the other of the narrow gap. Silent lurched as one piece of hot lead cut across his upper left arm, ripping his sleeve.

The lurch saved him, for the next ricochet sliced air bare inches from his jaw. He flung himself forward over the panicked claybank's head, rolling down and just missing being bitten by those large yellow teeth. He hit the ground hard enough to make him grunt and he rolled swiftly aside as the horse lunged forward, almost trampling him.

The man beyond rose in his stirrups, trying to glimpse Silent through the roiling dust. Silent spun on to his belly, bringing his rifle around awkwardly, the butt ploughing through the dirt. He fired and saw the chestnut lurch but the man wrenched the reins around and spurred away, dropping out of sight.

Silent's gun was empty again as he staggered up, trying to shuck fresh loads from his belt loops and get close enough to the frightened claybank to grab its reins.

It was a losing battle and the killer, whoever he was, got away. He sat down and waited for Gail to catch up, plastered with dirt, face smeared with dust and powder-smoke.

But at least she wasn't crying over that man she had shot. He was almost reluctant to bring her mind back to it, but said,

'Thanks. You saved my neck.'

Breathing hard from her climb, she half-turned and looked back to the far end of the ditch where the body sprawled. She stared in silence for a few moments, then turned to him and nodded slightly.

'I didn't even stop to think. It just seemed

like the thing to do.' Her voice was shaky.

'The only thing,' he assured her. 'Gail, you're getting used to how things are out here, whether you like it or not. Sometimes it has to be kill-or-be-killed – there's no other way.'

He was glad when her face straightened out and she nodded, again. 'I'll never get used to it, and I don't think I want to even try, but I couldn't let him kill you.' This time her voice was little more than a whisper.

'That's one I owe you.'

She frowned, snapped her head up. "Owe"? There's no favour involved here, no ... debt: I just reacted instinctively and – and–'

'Being the mighty fine rifle shot you are, you rid the world of a killer.'

'Perhaps I – evened it out – by saving you.'

He almost smiled. 'P'raps you did. Now wait here while I search that feller you nailed and then we'll decide what our next move will be.'

She said nothing, but groped her way to a boulder and sat down on it heavily, as if her legs were too weak to hold her. She watched without really seeing as he rummaged through the pockets of the dead man.

'Did you recognize the other rider? The

one who got away?'

He hesitated, glancing over his shoulder. 'Not sure. Think he was with Blackie when we were ambushed earlier. Which would make him Ralls. The brain behind the whole bloody business.'

CHAPTER 10

A GLIMPSE INTO HELL

There was nothing of interest in the dead man's pockets except an envelope addressed to 'P. Dish, General Delivery, Bisbee, Arizona Territory'. The return address was a scrawl but looked to both Silent and Gail like *Pedro Mining Co., Tucson*, followed by a private post office box number, half-smeared and barely legible.

There was no letter in the crumpled envelope and Silent guessed 'Dish' had saved it only for the full mining company address. Well, he wouldn't be needing it now.

'I'd like to see that letter.' Gail looked quizzically at Silent as he made the remark. 'I've heard of Packer Dish, a gun for hire, outlaw. Be good to know why a big mining company like San Pedro would be interested in the likes of him.'

Gail nodded slowly. 'You're thinking the company itself is involved? Someone high up working for them?'

He shrugged, folding the envelope into his shirt pocket. She had bandaged his arm where the bullet had creased him and the sleeve was torn, hung in a ragged flap.

'They mine gold as well as silver. Might be best if you go back to St David, Gail.' She stiffened at the suggestion and he added, 'Tell Lyall what's happened.'

'You, of course, will continue to track the man you think may be Ralls?' He nodded. 'And you consider this too dangerous for me?'

His dark eyes held her gaze, seeing the anger rising.

'If we're getting near the top of this thing, it'll be a lot more dangerous than it has been so far.'

'Thinking of the trail of dead men, I find that hard to believe.' Her mouth tightened. 'If you're doing this, believing I can't handle it...'

He shook his head. 'That's not it. I'm best working alone. Something like this, if I get a lead, I can act on it.'

'Without having to worry about me!'

He nodded curtly.

'I didn't realize I was such a burden to you.'

'Don't get persnicketty and come over all

132

hurt and teary. You're good to have along. You've done well so far.'

'But this's far enough!'

'For now.'

'I won't go! You can't make me. I have as much of a stake in this as you. My father died in that stagecoach massacre, or had you forgotten?'

'Nope. But I get these killers and your father's'll be among 'em.'

She thought about that, stiffened again. He made an exasperated motion but she spoke sharply. 'You're trying to salve my conscience!'

'Only you can do that.'

'No! You think I won't be able to handle it if I do actually kill my father's murderer! Well, I assure you–'

'You'll handle it OK. You're a lot tougher than you think. Than I think, wouldn't wonder.'

She was fighting a feeling of mollification that wanted to spread through her. 'Then why won't you take me with you?'

'Told you, I work best alone.'

'And I'd cramp your style! For killing!'

He merely stared at her. She pursed her lips and threw up her hands. 'I don't really have any choice, do I? I'm essentially a townswoman. You know the wilderness. You could lose me any time you wanted.'

'Any time.'

'Damn you!' She turned to her horse swiftly and mounted, glaring down at him. 'I hope Lyall gets a posse together and comes after you! *That'll* upset your "loner" image.'

'Might be he'll arrive in time to help finish it.'

'Oh! I wish I knew a lot of cuss-words like the trail men use, but I've had a sheltered upbringing. The best I can manage is simply another *damn you!*'

He smiled as she wrenched her mount around and started to spur away.

'Good as any, Gail!' He called as loud as his constricting throat would allow him.

The trail was leading him towards Tombstone but he had expected that.

Ralls – he had decided that's who he was following – seemed to be something more than a trouble-shooter for the stageline, masquerading as an agent. Or perhaps the mining company. They owned the stage-line as well, after all.

Just as he had figured he was heading directly into Tombstone, the trail took a swing to the west and south, towards the

San Pedro River. Beyond lay Huachuca City and, further south again, Sierra Vista. Neither was regularly served by the stage-lines but there were swing-stations where passengers could arrange to board. This was wild country, full of renegade Indians and outlaws, a stamping-ground for illegal whiskey-peddlers and gun-runners. Which meant there were a lot of hard-cases handy should a man feel in need of hiring their talents. For ambush. And the murder stage had been sighted in this general area.

Reading it that way, Silent decided that Ralls could be luring him into a trap, so he continued on towards Tombstone.

The town was no nest of fairies, either, but there were at least two large stageline depots there.

He rode in at mid-morning, circling north and coming in at a slant as if from the east. He could say he had travelled up from Bisbee, arriving like that. But Tombstone was a place of drifters – hardcases by the dozens, buffalo hunters in from the plains, a handful of Indians, usually some representatives of the army, trail-herders, prospectors, some down on their luck, others celebrating a bonanza. No one was likely to notice him if he waited until a few such riders were arriving and he trailed in close behind, as if part of the bunch, just travelling more slowly.

This was how he did it and no one took any particular notice when he set his trail-stained roan through the door of the OK Corral stables on Allen Street.

The heyday of the Earps in Tombstone was over although the ongoing feud with the Clanton–McLaury factions continued spasmodically after the explosive showdown at the OK Corral. The corral was on the far side of the block to the stables, corner of Third Street and Fremont, next to Fly's photographic studio. Tom and Frank McLaury and Billy Clanton were killed and, on the Earps' side, Virgil and Morgan were wounded, Doc Holliday received little more than a scratch and bruiser Wyatt escaped unharmed.

Less than a month later Virgil was crippled for life by an unknown assailant who blasted him with a shotgun. Five months after that, in March 1882, Morgan was shot in the back and killed while playing pool. Wyatt later killed a man he claimed was the murderer. But the Earp grip on Tombstone was loosening rapidly and Wyatt had drifted on, still hunting some of Morgan's killers, before Silent Wolf rode in.

He steered clear of the law office, didn't even know who was now town marshal. John Behan had been appointed sheriff and the word was he had a virtual army of deputies, determined to impose his will on the town and finish Wyatt Earp any way he knew how. Silent didn't care about the politics as long as he didn't tangle with those hard-horse deputies.

He had a little trouble finding a room and afterwards, when buying a new shirt, asked for directions to the San Pedro stage depot.

The counterman told him Wells Fargo had the biggest stageline offices, just a bit further along Allen Street. But Silent said no, he wanted the San Pedro line, and the man told him how to get there. Then the man began to ask what he apparently thought were casual questions about Silent's reason for wanting a stageline that hadn't another passenger coach scheduled before Saturday – three days off. Silent avoided a direct answer but suspected there was more behind the questions than just idle curiosity. He cursed his still-hoarse voice – it was a dead giveaway if Ralls had friends here on the lookout for him.

He walked past the stage depot, turned down a narrow street beside the building, saw a couple of men doing repairs on two Concord coaches. A third man, burly and obviously the workshop foreman, walked across to Silent where he stood looking in the doorway.

'Out of bounds here, feller. This street don't lead nowhere but to vacant land behind the depot. You musta took a wrong turn.'

Silent nodded. 'Guess so,' he agreed briefly, hoping the harshness of his voice didn't show up in those two short words. He moved back towards the main street. When he turned the corner he saw that the burly man was watching him. It wasn't all that unusual: there were tools in that workshop that would fetch a good price, coachwood and varnishes and paints, all easily converted to cash for a man who didn't mind taking a risk to steal them in the first place.

But he had an uneasy feeling that he was being watched, perhaps because of his trail-bum appearance and the fact that he was carrying his rifle unsheathed. There were plenty of others just like him, though without the raspy voice.

The information that there was a vacant lot behind the stage depot was worth remembering, though.

He was drinking his second beer with a whiskey chaser in Bob Hatch's saloon – now Bentinck's – where Morgan Earp had been killed, before the barkeep commented on his raspy voice. The man, hair plastered across his scalp in an effort to hide fast-encroaching baldness, gestured to Silent's scarred throat.

'Looks like your last whore was a cannibal.' He smiled when he spoke.

Silent moved his own lips a fraction in the suggestion of a smile. 'Can give you her name if you like.'

The 'keep shook his head. 'No, sir! I turn up with scars like that an' my Old Lady would reach for the meat cleaver. Lookin' for work?'

'Not right away.'

'Oh?' The man lowered his voice. 'Struck it rich back in the Dragoons, maybe?'

'Think I'd tell you?'

The barkeep's face sobered, then he forced a grin. 'Just makin' talk. You look a mite ... different from the other drifters.' When Silent said nothing, but only sipped his beer, the man added, 'Like you know what you want already.'

'Don't you? A hill of silver, a pretty woman and a saloon to drink dry all by myself.'

The barman laughed. 'You ain't so different! But you might like to leave that rifle someplace. The deputies don't like naked guns in town.'

Silent hefted the weapon. 'I'll take it to my room.'

'Where you stayin'?' The barkeep mopped the counter, trying to act as if only making conversation.

'Some rooming house. Never noticed the name.'

'How'll you find your way back? You like to describe it, I'll likely recognize it and–'

Silent lifted his rifle off the bar and the man had to jerk his head back away from the barrel.

'Hey! Judas, man, just tryin' to be friendly.'

'Too blamed friendly.'

Silent left and wandered around town past the Birdcage Theatre and the offices of John Clum's *Tombstone Epitaph* and ate a reasonable meal at the Lucky Cuss restaurant. He kept up his apparently aimless sightseeing and was pretty sure that two men who kept appearing at places to which he went – though not together – were following him. One had ginger hair, the other had dark, stubbled jowls.

He drifted around without hurry and saw signs of the men growing restless and bored with his meanderings. He sat in on a card game at the Crystal Palace where Wyatt Earp once ran a faro concession. It was a small-stake deal, which suited him, and his two followers, at opposite ends of the saloon, were soon bored and left. No excitement there.

He tossed in his hand and went out through a side door. The ginger-haired man was standing at the end of the boardwalk, building a cigarette. The other man was not in sight so Silent waited until the ginger-haired man had lit his smoke and stepped down from the walk. He followed him at a distance, slowing by every doorway and alley entrance so that he could step in quickly if the man turned around.

But he wasn't quite fast enough, slipping into an alley on Toughnut Street where there were miners' cabins and even the entrance to an operating mine itself: the Goodenough. He had seen the ginger-haired man slowing down at the fire station and start to turn casually. Silent stepped hurriedly into the alley near another mine entrance, the Million Dollar Stope, still trying to keep an eye on Ginger, who seemed to have gone into the fire station now.

Then he felt a gun muzzle scrape his spine and a deep voice said, 'Time we met and had a talk, mister ... I'll take that.'

A hairy-wristed hand reached around Silent for his rifle and he spun quickly, bringing the barrel up at an angle, ramming it deep into the man's belly. It was the dark-haired man with the heavy stubble he had been seeing behind him all day wherever he went. Like he had said, it was time to talk.

The man gagged, knees sagging. Silent clipped him across the side of the head with the rifle butt, then Ginger came charging at him from the other end of the alley and was upon him before he could get the rifle gripped properly again. A Colt barrel struck the gun from his grip, then swung back-handed at Silent's head.

He jerked away, punched Ginger's gun arm, striking hard and sending the man off balance. As Ginger staggered, dropping his six-gun, Silent stepped in and hammered a barrage of fast blows at the man's weaving head – left, left, left, setting him up for a straight right that travelled no more than a foot. His knuckles cracked against the man's jaw. Ginger faltered and his legs buckled. He stumbled, fighting for balance, and Silent went after him.

But the black-stubbled man had recovered enough to put in his two cents' worth. His fist drove against Silent's kidneys and he staggered. Ginger, though dazed, clawed at him, managed to pin Silent's arms in a bear hug. Helpless, though struggling, Silent saw the tight grin on the dark man's face an instant before a gun barrel took him across the side of the head. Ginger flung him violently away and watched him stretch out on the alley floor amongst the accumulated rubbish, barely conscious.

He kicked Silent in the side and the dark one pulled him away.

'You know what Ralls said. Bring him in, but in talkin' condition.'

Ginger wiped his bleeding nostrils and spat on the dazed, moaning Silent. 'Grab his shoulders, then. I'll take his feet,' he growled, kicking Silent's rifle under the low building of the mine office, amongst even more rubbish.

Someone threw cold water over him and the shock brought him round, gasping and spluttering.

It took a few moments before his eyes focused and he saw he was in a clapboard shack with an earthen floor. A small table about two feet square had a burning lamp on it, and there were a few chairs. A man was seated in one of these. The two men who had jumped Silent in the alley stood close to the chair he was now tied to, arms roped through the back. A dripping pail stood beside Ginger's legs.

The man behind the table had to be Ralls. He wore a brown corduroy coat, a silk vest that had seen better days and Silent could just make out the *buscadero* gun belt above the edge of the table. The butts of the twin guns looked like staghorn. There was a heavy silver ring on the hand that rested on the table beside a shot glass of reddish liquid.

The dull lamplight threw highs and shadowed lows on a hard-planed face, a sharp jaw making the man's features appear triangular. Colourless hair was brushed back in thick natural waves around ears with large lobes.

'So you're the one they call "Silent".'

Silent demonstrated his nickname in the best way he knew how. Ralls smiled thinly.

'A suitable answer. Why're you bothering the hell outta me and my associates?'

'Didn't Bowdrie tell you? The guard he

cut up was my kid brother.'

Ralls's face straightened and then he nodded gently. 'We thought the Chiricahuas had gotten rid of you. I can savvy how you feel. You want Will Bowdrie in particular?'

'You offering? I've already killed Zack.'

The finger with the heavy ring lifted briefly. 'No need to remind me. Pity, that. Zack was a good man.'

'He is now.'

Ginger made a growling sound but Ralls's smile widened. 'Sassy son of a bitch, ain't you. Well, makes no nevermind. Now I know what you're after there're two things I can do to get rid of you: kill you or give you Will Bowdrie.'

Both Ginger and the dark-stubbled man came off the wall, outraged. Ginger protested sharply.

'Just a minute, Ralls! Will's a pard of mine!'

'By God, you throw him to the wolves, what'd you do with the likes of us?' This last was from the stubbled man.

Ralls's flat, cold eyes swung to him. 'Jace, you have more brains than I gave you credit for. Hell, I was joshing. There's only one way to handle this ranny with his voice like he's got a throatful of broken glass. *Hey!*

Someone can *give* him a throatful and toss him in the river.'

Ginger and Jace both smiled. 'Now that's better!'

'We have the job?' Jace was eager.

Ralls seemed to think about that, then nodded. 'Why not? Guess even a couple of rummies could handle that chore without making a mess of it.'

'Er – bonus...?' asked Jace, hopefully.

Ralls's eyes narrowed, but then he nodded, a single jerky movement. 'Silent, I'm wondering just how much you know. You've been on our necks for weeks and from what I've seen of you, you're mighty dangerous.'

'Ask Sheriff Lyall in St David,' Silent rasped and he saw Ralls stiffen. 'He knows what I know.'

The man closed his fist around the shot glass and, keeping his bleak stare on the prisoner, tossed down the drink quickly. 'I think that's a bluff. But there's too much at stake here to risk it. Ginger, Jace, before you start breaking bottles and ramming the glass down his throat, do a little work on him: you know, a cut here, a broken bone there, maybe. See how much he really knows. I don't want that sonuver Lyall buying into this deal.'

The two hardcases were happy as Ralls stood and took down a curl-brim hat from a nail hammered into the wall. He made for a door just visible beyond the throw of the lamplight, paused with a hand on the latch.

'Before you finish him, report to me what he's told you. And no shooting: I don't want the damn deputies coming.'

'Where'll you be?' Jace asked.

'Try Bentink's – someone there'll know.'

He went out and the two men turned to Silent who was straining futilely against his ropes.

'Turn up the lamp, Jace. I wanna see his face while I change its shape.'

Ginger tugged on a pair of leather work-gloves and went to stand before Silent. His lips stretched tightly over his large teeth.

'Pul-eeease live up to your name, Silent. We ain't in no hurry to hear you talk. Fact, longer you take, the better we'll like it, eh, Jace?'

'Get on with it! I want my turn, too.'

He coughed in the black smoke rising from the cracked glass chimney of the lamp and pulled Silent's chair closer to the table so they could see his suffering more clearly.

Shouldering each other out of the way, they began, taking it in turns to beat Silent.

The punches had a lot of power behind them and the chair overbalanced more than once.

They were lifting it back to an even keel for the third time when Silent, his legs not bound to the chair, swung up his boots against the edge of the table.

It lifted a few inches off the floor. The lamp overturned and shattered, spreading a sheet of burning oil against the warped, weathered boards of the old miner's shack.

Flames flared, spreading swiftly, as if a window had opened to give them a glimpse into hell.

CHAPTER 11

HELL ON TWO FEET

Ginger stumbled against the burning wall and let out a scream of terror as his clothes caught fire. He clawed away, shouting, slapping at one sleeve and the back of his shirt.

Jace snatched up the pail that still had some water in it, tossed it over his pard, but was caught in a swirl of choking smoke. He coughed and his eyes watered. Doubled over, he snatched off his neckerchief and held it to his face, groping for the door, bent almost double.

Hurting and half-conscious, Silent lay on his side on the earthen floor, still tied to his overturned chair. He tripped Ginger as the man lurched to his feet, one sleeve still smouldering, the rest extinguished. Ginger swore, kicked at him and drew his pistol.

'No shootin', Ralls said!' choked Jace, opening the door and tumbling out.

Ginger snarled, stomped at Silent's head,

missed, but his boot splintered the back of the chair. 'Burn, you bastard!'

He swung away, groping for the door now in the heavy smoke filling the room. Jace was already out and they could hear miners in the main block of cabins down the hill shouting and running up here. The possibility of fire among the old shacks was no pleasant thing to contemplate.

Silent struggled and the broken chair-back gave way so that he could at least get free of it, though his wrists were still roped behind him. The air was clearer down at floor level and he crawled to the table, then struggled to his knees. He used his feet to turn the table on to its side. Straining, coughing, he worked two of the legs under his bound arms, one each side of his chest, sliding them beneath his armpits. Clamping his arms tight, he lurched upright, the table top sagging in front like a cumbersome battering ram.

Head lowered, eyes closed, he floundered forward, staggered and fell to one knee as the heavy table top smashed into, then through, the flimsy burning planks. He felt as though a horse had kicked him. He let the table drop and it rolled swiftly away from the blazing wall. Men were milling about now outside and a couple ran forward and dragged him clear.

'Hell, he's tied up!'

'Get me ... free,' Silent rasped and they hesitated.

'Why you hogtied?' one asked, but he produced a clasp knife and began to saw at the ropes.

'A prank that went wrong.' Silent knew it was a feeble explanation, but he didn't aim to stick around answering questions. There was quite a crowd now and he pushed into it, rubbing his forearms and hands briskly to restore circulation, edging away all the time. Someone had started a bucket brigade and they concentrated on this.

He looked for Ginger and Jace, saw them in the crowd, staring towards the broken-through wall as it burned. The discarded chair was clearly visible and burning in the light of the flames. Soon they would be searching for him and this time they would shoot on sight, risking the wrath of Ralls and the deputies. He was unarmed and hatless.

He had little trouble in making his way down the hill, getting below the crowd. By that time he was able to feel his hands almost normally. Two deputies had arrived to take charge. His throat and lungs were raw from the smoke. He smothered a series of coughs. Panting, he reached the foot of the slope, keeping away from where the lawmen tried to organize the jostling crowds as more townsfolk arrived.

He sidled alongside a building and a tall plank fence, then realized this was right next to the alley where he had been jumped.

Waiting his chance for a break in the sight-seers, he hurried along the boardwalk and turned into the alley. The first thing he did was step on something soft and he reached down warily, grinned when he found it was his hat, which had been knocked off during the earlier brawl. He punched it out and jammed it on his head, foolishly feeling better because of it. Cowboys and the myth of their hats! But it was comforting...

Then, on hands and knees, he groped warily just beneath the clapboard skirt of the low building, scraping rubbish aside, jumping when he touched a squealing rat. But he also touched the stock of his rifle. He snatched up the weapon and, crouching, ran down the alley to a vacant lot. His legs became entangled in the weeds as he floundered his way on, parallel with Allen Street, though one block over.

Just around the corner were the OK Corral stables where his roan was stalled. There was a spare Colt in the saddle-bags that he had left attached to his rig. Hurrying down Third Street to Allen, a brief scout showed him the livery was empty, everyone out at the fire, no doubt. He went in, got the six-gun and checked its loads before ramming it into his holster. He saddled the roan and led it back to the intersection with Third, leaving it with reins trailing in a dark corner of a vacant lot that continued on behind the line of buildings; these included the offices of the San Pedro Stageline.

There was no one around and it took him only moments to force open the rear door and grope his way into the small cubicle where the records clerk would normally work. No one was in the workshop. He drew the drapes across the only window, lit a tallow candle in a tin holder and set about checking the tagged name cards on the filing cabinets. The mountain of papers was daunting but whoever clerked for the stageline was methodical and he found the section he was after faster than he could have hoped.

The departure dates of the stage that had cost Larry his life were burned into his brain. He riffled through the papers, found the date when the Tombstone run had arrived before heading north again.

He frowned. These records had to be false! If he believed them, going by the dates, it took the stage almost three days to make the turn-around before heading north. No stageline could operate on such a timetable, but...

Those three days would cover a run to Huachuca and back, with time to spare – and *that* item was not listed anywhere. *Picking up the gold from the old mines...?*

Actually, nothing had ever been mentioned about which direction the stage had been travelling in when ambushed. Like everyone else, he had assumed it was on the way south and no one had told him any different. Not that it made any real difference. A hurried search showed him that the dead passengers on the list had boarded here, in Tombstone or *earlier in Bisbee*. And the dates matched with Gail's sighting of Larry in that border town. Then the stage had been driven to that arroyo near St David and the massacre had taken place, leaving fake signs of renegade Indians...

One of the passengers was the San Pedro mine manager, Pat Sievers, who was murdered along with the others. If he was supposed to be manager of the mine's head office in Tucson, what had he been doing down here?

Overseeing the secret shipment of gold, maybe?

Hands shaking slightly, he checked something else: the shotgun guard was listed as 'Larry Clay – new man in training'.

Worksheets were attached and Larry's neat signature jumped out at him from among the scrawls and scratchings of other stageline employees. Slowly running a finger back across the line where Larry's name was, he saw the notation in the column marked 'Previous Run' as 'Tombstone/Bisbee, Run No 231'.

So what were you guarding on stagecoach Number 231, little brother? If anything...

It took more time than he wanted to spend, but he traced the details of 231's trip from Tombstone to Bisbee, designated as 'Special Itinerary – Arizona Union.'

He wondered what 'Arizona Union' meant, as he ran his finger down the list, looking for more information. The stage had carried two boxes of telegraphic message keys with hook-ups, brass posts, arms and bases, including replacement pins and clamps, twelve in each box; two large coils of heavy-gauge copper wire, presumably also for the telegraph office; a gross of cotter pins for coach-wheel hubs; four iron hand levers with brake-blocks attached, including bolts and nuts; two sets of driving-seat handrails; and several assortments of harness buckles. Everything made of metal, and heavy, bound for the Arizona Union Mercantile *and Smeltery* in Bisbee.

'By God, 231 must've been bending its springs down to the ground with that load, plus passengers.'

But these were goods that hardly required the presence of a shotgun guard! There was nothing else of real value on the bill of lading: a couple of small crates of perishables, bolts of fabric, barbers' haircutting instruments, the usual bundles of magazines and some out-of-date Eastern and West Coast newspapers.

'Must've sent Larry just to gain some experience,' he decided. 'It would show as "training" on the records.'

But damned expensive. There had to be another reason. He quickly looked at the lading bill again.

'Hell! Arizona Mercantile *and Smeltery...*!'

And then the street door burst open and Ralls stood there with a gun in his hand, Ginger and Jace behind.

'I *told* you the son of a bitch would get out of that shack!' Ralls brought up his six-gun but he shouldn't have taken time to vindicate himself with his hardcases first.

Silent swept the candle to the floor, plunging the room into darkness. Crouched, rifle braced into his hip, he worked lever and trigger, filling the room with flashing thunder – and flying splinters and bullets.

The trio shouted and he heard them scrabbling for cover as he ran out through the back door and across the vacant lot. He hadn't gone far when guns banged behind him but he didn't hear any bullets flying close.

He made his way around to the vacant lot where the saddled roan browsed on the weeds. Most of the town was still up the hill, making sure the fire didn't spread to the inhabited miners' cottages, but the gunfire was bound to bring the law.

He found the roan, quickly reloaded the rifle and turned to mount as gunfire thudded in a wild volley. The roan whickered and quivered but didn't seem to be hurt. Silent spotted Jace and Ginger, running in at an angle, a good distance between them so he could only shoot at one at a time.

He brought the rifle to his shoulder with a

swift, certain movement, triggered almost instantly. Ginger was hurled back, boots clear of the ground, arms spreading wide before he fell in a limp pile. Jace swore and dropped flat as Silent's lead kicked dirt and gravel into his face. He clawed at his eyes, momentarily blinded, and then Silent was in the saddle, crouching low as he spurred the roan across the weeds. Two more men were running towards him with guns out, one a sawn-off shotgun, and specks of bright, reflected light from the left sides of their shirtfronts. *Badge-toters!*

Earning curses but uncaring, Silent weaved through the fringes of the gawking crowds and cleared town for the Bisbee trail in a few minutes. A shotgun thundered but he knew the deputy would have fired the sawed-off into the air, not risking hitting any townsmen.

He glanced behind, didn't see any signs of actual pursuit. But he knew damn well it would be there – just as soon as Ralls could get it organized.

'Who *is* that hellion?' demanded the deputy with the smoking shotgun, replacing the shell he had fired. He threw the question at Ralls who was standing over Ginger's body. He looked up bleakly. Jace came up warily.

'Calls himself "Silent" because he can't talk in much more than a whisper. Real name's Aaron Clay. He's involved in that stagecoach massacre up north,' Ralls said easily. 'I've been expecting him to show. He's already killed a couple of my men up there. He thinks there was gold on board and aims to grab it.'

The deputy, a hard-eyed man of about forty, said, 'Lot of folk think there was secret gold on that stage.'

'Well, they hid it damn well if there was,' Ralls said curtly. 'And I ought to know. Listen, you gonna get a posse up? I want that killer run down!'

'Yeah. Know where he's headed?'

Ralls smiled crookedly. 'Only one place – Bisbee.'

'He won't get far.' The deputy turned to his sidekick. 'Posse, Ned. Ten men minimum – for Bisbee.'

That was what Ralls wanted to hear.

Gail Cobb was far from satisfied with Sheriff Lyall's reaction to her suggestion that he should form a posse.

He clutched a worn robe about him and was obviously quite ill. 'Doc says I've got more than concussion, mebbe a small fracture, and I won't argue with him,' the grey-faced sheriff told Gail. He leaned in the doorway of his living quarters beside the jail-house. She could hear his wife moving about in the background. 'Can't see properly, sick to my boots. Want to sleep all the time.'

'I sympathize with you, Sheriff, but what about Silent?'

'Aaron Clay,' he corrected her, slurring, face hardening some, but he gripped the edge of the door more tightly. 'I done some searching through my dodgers. He's not named, but there's one where the description comes mighty close – horse-stealing, up in the Dakotas, man shot down.'

Gail stiffened. 'You – you can't hound him on just a description that *might* fit! That's hardly fair!'

'Lyall, will you get in here? You're not even s'posed to be out of bed!'

The woman's voice was querulous and Lyall winced.

'I'm in no mood to worry about "fair". Clay's trouble, any way you look at him. I've sent telegrams to Tombstone and the marshal in Bisbee. He'll pick up Clay and hold him till it's decided one way or another.'

Gail gasped, frowning. 'You – old – fool! Once they get him in a cell, he's a sitting duck! They'll kill him!'

'Marshal Kelty's a good man – he won't let that happen. Now, I'm crawling back to bed, Miss Cobb. 'Night.'

He closed the door on Gail as his wife called for him to come in *at once!*

CHAPTER 12

ON THE DODGE

The Tombstone deputy was wrong when he said Silent wouldn't get far. He was many miles ahead of the posse.

Too confident, the hastily formed band rode out of town and hit the trail for Bisbee. They didn't even stop to check for tracks. This bothered Ralls some but Jace was ready to go along with the lawmen. Ginger had been his pard and he wanted to square things with Silent. *Pronto.*

To do that, however, the posse should have been riding due south, but this direction never occurred to them. They stuck to the regular Bisbee trail as if it was the only way Silent would go. Deputy Ray Dancey, the posse's head man, ordered an occasional scout to either side of the main trail, and didn't seem very concerned when no sign of Silent was reported.

'We should've found some sign!' complained Ralls.

Dancey gave Ralls a flinty stare. 'You want to spend a few hours, sure, we'll pick up somethin', but it'd be wasted time. He'll use this trail to Bisbee. Fastest way.'

Well, it seemed that that was Dancey's decision, but Ralls was mighty uneasy and dropped back a little with Jace as the noisy posse men continued on.

'That son of a bitch is smarter than Dancey allows. I figure he's stayin' clear of the regular trail. So where would he go and still get to Bisbee in a reasonable time?'

'He could cut across to Elfrida, then drop south,' Jace said slowly, not sounding convincing.

'No.' Ralls dismissed it curtly. 'Too slow and far. Too many places he could be spotted. How about due south?'

Jace stiffened. 'Hell, that's nothin' country, bare as a shorn lamb. Not even good water.'

'But where would it take him?' Ralls insisted.

'Only to the border. Nothin' between here and there, and if he followed the river – *Judas!* He could cross into Mexico and turn back north to Naco and practic'ly *spit* into Bisbee's main street!'

'Get moving, Jace.'

Jace hesitated: he had seen what Silent

could do and Ginger was dead to prove it. He licked dry lips. 'You comin'?'

Ralls shook his head. 'I'll hang with this bunch. I want to find Silent dead when we reach Bisbee. If his body's never found, so much the better.' As he saw Jace was still hesitant, he added, with a touch of bitterness, 'There'll be an extra five hundred in it for you.'

That decided Jace and he dropped back until he trailed the posse, then ran his mount for a large boulder field, swinging due south – towards the distant border.

By sun-up Silent had a good lead and he stopped by a low butte, carefully keeping rocks between him and the north as he checked the country through field glasses.

No sign of the posse.

He didn't underestimate Ralls, or the lawmen, even though he knew neither well. But they were professionals and when no one found sign of him heading for Bisbee after the first couple of miles out from Tombstone where he had deliberately left tracks, someone was bound to think about Silent going by way of the border.

So far it looked as though they were simply charging along the regular Bisbee trail. *Lots of luck, fellas!*

They would get to Bisbee before him, most likely, but that was OK. He could slip in after dark and check out a few things, then do what he had to.

When he left Bisbee there would be some men bound for Boot Hill.

It never occurred to him – or didn't matter a damn, if it did – that he could be one of them.

Jace Woodring had a good horse under him and, urged on by the thought of an extra $500, he pushed it hard on the way south. He had started to angle west towards the San Pedro River, but figured this would only add miles to the journey and Silent would avoid that.

What Jace wanted to do was not just catch up with Silent, but to get ahead and set up an ambush. He was pretty fast with a six-gun and a tolerable rifle shot, but he did his best work when he was lying prone, rifle on a steady rest of rock or a Y-fork branch cut from a bush.

A long, easy sighting, making allowances for wind and sun-flashes, even unexpected eddies of dust – and his man was dead in the blink of an eye.

'And five hundred in my pocket!' he said aloud, feeling the excitement stir his blood. He raked with his spurs, drove his mount slightly west, swung around a mound of big boulders that looked liked the backs of a herd of feeding dinosaurs. He hesitated – should he ride in, climb atop one of those granite eggs and search for Silent's dust? Or keep riding fast, try to overtake the man, get around him, or above him; back-shooting presented no problem to Jace Woodring.

He chose the boulder mound, cursing the horse as it protested, weary and badly treated. Jace forced the mount into the field, weaved between the rocks, searching for the tallest and most accessible.

In the shadow of the huge rock, Jace reined in and was reaching for his rifle in the scabbard under his right leg when he froze: there was a movement breaking the arched line of the big boulder. Heart thudding up into his throat, he snapped his head up and swallowed when he saw it was Silent, standing there with boots spread.

It looked as though his rifle and some field glasses were lying at his feet and Jace swore softly. Of course! The biggest, easiest boulder in the field! Why the hell wouldn't Silent choose it as his lookout, too?

'Didn't think you had the brains to figure I'd be on this trail, Jace.' The rasping words seemed even more contemptuous because of their whispering sound, bouncing raggedly off the rocks.

'You ain't got no monopoly on horse-sense, mister!'

'Climb down.'

Jace bristled but forced down his fear-driven anger. 'Why the hell should I?'

Silent shrugged. 'Die in the saddle then.'

That startled Jace and he tumbled out of leather, one leg folding under him as he lunged away from the horse, reaching for his six-gun. He didn't even see Silent's hand move, but flame stabbed from it and Jace felt the hammer-blow high in his body. An instant later there was the shock of the bullet shattering his shoulder blade on the way through. It flung him violently to the ground and he sobbed in pain, his half-drawn Colt falling from his holster.

But Jace was no longer interested. He lay there, gasping and moaning, left hand clawing into the bleeding wound. Silent hunkered down atop his boulder.

'I shoot your horse, you're in one helluva bind, Jace.'

'You – you think I – ain't – already?'

Silent slid down over the boulder's rough curve. He stumbled when he reached the ground but Woodring was no danger to him now. Jace was too wrapped up in his own pain. He looked up with fear in his eyes as Silent towered over him, still holding the smoking Colt.

'Posse somewheres back there?'

'F – find – out!'

Silent nodded, hunkering down beside the wounded man. He pushed back his hat, the shadow lifting and exposing his dirt-grained, dust-smeared face, the red-rimmed eyes and, most of all, perhaps, the hard unbending line of his mouth.

'I aim to, Jace. You just yell "'nuff!" when you feel like it.'

Jace, breathing hard, fighting pain and waves of dizziness, watched as Silent holstered his Colt and drew out his clasp knife. He opened the blade with his teeth, tested it on his thumb, shook his head briefly.

'Too blunt,' he said in that blood-chilling whisper. 'I don't care about the extra pain you'd suffer, me having to saw away with a blunt blade, but I'm pushed for time, Jace.'

He picked up a wind-smoothed stone and spat onto it, began to hone the drop-point blade, doing it carefully, testing the edge

168

from time to time. Jace cringed. Silent shaved a sliver of horny thumbnail and nodded in satisfaction. He hitched around and pushed the wounded man down onto his back.

Jace cried out. 'Jesus! Wha– what you gonna – do?'

'Guess.'

'No! No, wait! I had nothin' to do with – your bro – brother! That was – the Bowdries – Bodine held him.'

Silent moved only his dark, hellish eyes. 'They had to make it look like he'd been tortured, as if someone was trying to make him tell where the gold was. That it?'

Chest heaving, face corpselike now, Jace nodded as vigorously as he could.

'Who – gave – that – order?' Silent asked clearly.

Jace didn't answer. He looked as though he wanted to scream, but there was some kind of conflict in his brain right now and he couldn't even force out a cry of fear. Silent leaned forward, placing the blade against Jace's nose which was greasy with sweat.

'Ever see a man without a nose, Jace? I haven't. Seen a squaw or two, though. Injuns cut off their wives' noses if they catch 'em with another buck. The look of it's

169

enough to spoil a grizzly's appetite. I'll try to do yours without too much sawing and hacking.'

'Ralls!' The word exploded out of Jace's twisted mouth and he seemed to collapse in on himself, sobbing. 'It was – Ralls! He's – he's the head – troubleshooter...'

He retched noisily, and Silent stood slowly, allowing the sun to blaze a bar of light from the knife blade into Jace's terror-filled eyes. 'Who gives him orders?'

It was too late now. Jace knew he was already a dead man, even if by some miracle he survived this afternoon with whispering death hovering over him. Once they knew he'd talked...

'Was Pat Sievers.'

'Mine manager? He was killed in the massacre, wasn't he?'

Jace nodded wearily. 'Ralls done it. Figured folk'd – think Pat was ridin' along – to keep an eye on the – gold everyone figured they knew – was – there – but wasn't. Aimed for Pat to be the only survivor. He'd take in word about – the raid, be a kinda hero to the company. But Ralls'd set him up, then killed him.'

'Smart. Let Sievers organize it all, then kill him and get a bigger share. Time for some details, Jace.'

He gave the man some water and Woodring told all he knew.

Seemed the San Pedro mine had worked gold as well as silver, which was common enough in the Dragoon mineral belt. Sievers and Ralls had gotten together and doctored the company reports, downgrading the output figures. With the connivance of some of the miners, it was easy enough to secretly ship out the raw gold, in freight boxes labelled as some fictitious, heavy merchandise, such as machine parts, stagecoach spares, telegraph key bases and so on. With the co-operation of Ralls, who managed the mine's other business interest in southeastern Arizona – the San Pedro Stageline – it was a breeze.

'Head office had no idea they was bein' robbed of a fortune. They trusted Pat.'

'Sievers shipped unaccounted-for mined gold to Bisbee under false bills of lading? Always marking the "goods" as something made of metal, so as to account for the weight in the boxes ... was that the idea?'

Jace nodded miserably. 'They – found some good pay dirt in one of them abandoned mines north of Huachuca, too. Worked that, told the company no dice.

Had a whole new bonus...'

'What went wrong?'

'Mine company decided to sell. Buyers wanted to send down their own geologists an' accountants to check it out.'

'And Sievers panicked.' Silent mused. Any geologist or mining engineer worth his salt would know by simply studying the vein whether it was yielding pay dirt or not. 'What'd Sievers do? Fake a report of one final, big gold shipment, making out the vein had produced a pocket worth real money at last. Then he set up the stage massacre so he could claim that the gold was stolen and he never would have to account for what he'd already taken! Smart move. Sievers should've been on stage as a magician.'

Jace nodded. 'It – it was workin' – fine. The geologists fell for it, so did the buyers. Then you turned up!'

'Cat among the pigeons. Got a habit of doing that.'

Silent closed the knife and Jace relaxed visibly when the blade clicked into its socket. 'Someone's got to pay for Larry. They used him as a pawn all along; a professional shotgun guard would suspect something was wrong with the set-up, so they hired a greenhorn, went through all the farce of "training" him. Then hacked him to pieces. Made it look like Apaches just to cloud the water.'

Silent's voice had strengthened, though he hadn't noticed. It was deep emotion forcing his thoughts out loud and the fierceness of the sound shook Woodring to his boots.

He was careful not to look at Silent's fearsome face now. His terror was complete; he couldn't stop wondering how he was going to die. Bullet? Blade? Dragged behind a horse on a rope till the skin flayed off his bones?

His imagination ran wild.

Silent stood slowly, looking down at the shaking man, and twisted his fingers in Jace's greasy hair, his other hand on his Colt butt. The gun was half-drawn as he stared down into those terror-stricken eyes, He growled once in frustration, *'Aaagh!'* and thrust Woodring from him roughly, pushing the man on to his side. Jace's cry of pain was cut off abruptly as he passed out, bladder voiding.

Silent unsaddled Jace's mount and slapped it on the rump, setting it running free with a whicker that could have been pleasure, relief, or simply contempt for these humans.

The posse would find it and backtrack. It would slow them down. Whether Jace Woodring would be still alive when they eventually found him ... well, that was Jace's gamble; he was lucky to get his chance.

Silent dragged the unconscious man into the shade and dumped his saddle and gear alongside him. He tore up a shirt taken from Woodring's saddlebags, wadded some strips over the entry wound, and tied it roughly. He left the rest beside Jace with the man's canteen.

Then Silent moved back into the boulder-field, whistling for the roan.

It was still a long way to Bisbee, and a lot of enemies would be waiting, eager to force the showdown he had been wanting for weeks.

Not before time, either.

CHAPTER 13

RED ANGEL

He had to keep to the west and make sure he stayed clear of the regular Tombstone–Bisbee trail. A dust cloud would be enough to bring in at least part of the posse to investigate.

When Jace didn't return someone would likely come looking, too, whether the riderless horse arrived or not. So he rode west, almost to within sight of the river, pushing the roan, but watching that he didn't overdo it. An exhausted horse was no damn good out here.

Apart from the natural hazards, there was always the risk of roving bands of 'Cherrycow' Apaches, just waiting to pounce on a lone rider; preferably a white man, but if there was a horse or mule involved the colour of the loner's skin wouldn't matter, anyway.

And, occasionally, there was danger from Mexican outlaw bands, the *declalar fueras*, cutting north in the hope of a quick kill and profit from some unsuspecting wanderer of the border wastelands, or a settler's lonely sod hut.

It was not his stamping ground, but he had been here before. Years ago. Then he had been riding on the fringes of a wild bunch that he had joined when they tangled with some Mexicans. Silent had happened along and his extra gun made the difference and saved the day. They didn't even have to ask him to join them. A bunch of 'Cherry-cows' had followed, watching for a couple of days, but eventually they dispersed and disappeared into the barren land after a buffalo-runner called Bison brought one down with a single shot from his Sharps Big-Fifty at a distance of half a mile.

Silent wouldn't mind such a gun – and the ability to mimic Bison's marksmanship – right now.

But he only had his battered, but well-oiled Winchester .44/.40 and the Colt with the walnut grip that had a crack in one of the butt-scales, which he kept meaning to fix. And he was low on ammunition.

What he had was likely enough to get him out of 'ordinary' trouble – whatever that might be! In addition he had a half-saddle canteen of warm water, some hardtack, and, for the moment at least, his health and all his faculties. *It had better be enough.*

Heat haze hurt his eyes and the dryness made his throat ache. The metal parts of his guns and harness were too hot to touch. The roan slowed noticeably, plodding through the fetlock-deep grey dust. Silent stopped, punched in the crown of his hat and spilled a couple of cupfuls of water into the hollow. The roan sucked it down in noisy slurps. Silent swilled his own mouth from the canteen, swallowing slowly.

He hawked and spat in an effort to free his throat of grit, then swung due east. There was no Rio Grande to mark the border here as there was in Texas. It was an imaginary line, nothing tangible to show where one country ended and another began, just a continuation of the wasteland. But somewhere ahead lay the trail to Naco, a border town of mixed nationality, predominantly Mexican.

The last time he was there he had saved a cantina prostitute from having her face torn open by the rowels of a drunken gringo's spurs. She had offered herself in gratitude, and added if ever he needed help of any kind, she and her brother, Chico, were at hand – he only had to ask.

Her name was Angelica Rojo, 'Red Angel'. A fanciful name, but she had been obsessed with red hair at that time and had eventually found a dye that gave her hair like fire. She believed it attracted men, both Anglo and Spanish, and maybe she was right because she was the most sought-after whore in her brother's cantina. It, too, was called the Red Angel. Chico had been grateful to Silent for saving his sister from disfigurement. But his gratitude had abruptly withered when the American law from Bisbee gave him a hard time. Silent, then known by his real name of Aaron Clay, had killed the spur-wielding gringo in a gunfight in the cantina. But it wasn't Chico who had suffered most from that encounter, though he blamed Silent for the trouble it had caused him.

Well, he knew no one else who might help him in this neck of the woods. He had to take a chance that Angelica was still here and still grateful, and that Chico and the law had forgiven him. How the hell was he to know the man with the spurs was an undercover marshal, working to break up a white-slave ring.

Silent was damn sure the man hadn't been acting when he threatened Angelica; he was just a mean, drunken bully. He had forced the gunfight and had died on the spot with Silent's bullet in his heart.

It had taken Silent a long time to get his neck out of a noose then, but the marshal, another mean son of a bitch named Kelty, had the last laugh. Refusing to admit it had been a fair gunfight, but unable to prove otherwise, he searched his wanted dodgers until he found one that named Aaron Clay as the killer of a man in another gunfight in another town, a year ago. Still bitter because Clay had upset his covert investigation, Kelty worked his butt off until, eventually, he saw Clay put away for two years on the rockpile in Yuma.

Well, all that was in the past, but he still had no great love for lawmen, whatever kind of badge they toted. Anyone interested enough could thank Kelty and his under-hand tricks for that. He hoped the man had moved on from Naco long ago.

He rode in at night, cantina music floating over the low-built adobe buildings. Activity was mainly concentrated in the south side of town, the red light district, closest to the border. Shadows moved within shadows. He felt many eyes watching as he dismounted at the hitchrail in the small plaza. The Red

Angel should be on his right, set back a few feet from the plaza, a brushwood *ramada*, with a few tables and chairs beneath, shading the arched entrance.

It was there, but the *ramada* was gone and there were batwings fitted to the entrance that used to be doorless. And now the name painted above it was simply, *Chico's*.

Must be the right place. Silent hitched his gun belt and used his rifle barrel to push open one side of the batwings before entering. It was smoky and noisy, two guitars strumming and straining to be heard. A plump girl with a grating, barrelhouse voice and frizzy hair, stood near the end of the bar, swaying as she mouthed some Spanish song. Two men were scuffling in a corner but not too seriously – at least no knives were out yet. The drinkers at other tables or just standing against the walls were mostly Mexican.

The girl finished her song, turned swiftly and rapped the bar. The man behind it, thirtyish, bullet-headed and bleak-eyed, slapped a glass of tequila on the woodwork, but his black eyes burned into Silent as he approached.

'*Buenos noches*, Chico,' he said, laying his rifle on the bartop, the movement causing drinkers nearby to shuffle away. 'Can I drink your tequila without doubling up as it eats my belly out?'

Chico's eyes narrowed. There was no doubt he recognized Silent. He kept his gaze on the tall *Americano* as he poured from a bottle he took from beneath the bar. 'Better than they serve in Yuma, Señor Clay.'

'So's puma piss.' Silent sipped, but the tequila was of reasonable quality. Still, the spirits burned his throat and he covered the glass with his hand as Chico made to refill it. 'We *amigos?*'

Chico was frowning. 'Your voice – it has changed.' He grinned suddenly. 'Maybe because you grow up, eh?'

'Yuma helps. You oughta try it sometime. *Amigos* or not, Chico?' He sounded indifferent but Chico guessed it was an act. He shrugged, flicked his eyes to the shadowed rear of the room and then back to Silent. 'I still have some *problemas* with the law because of you, but I am prosperous enough now to keep most of them small ones.' He rubbed thumb and forefinger together. 'It has taken a long time, and is still not totally settled. Sometimes I curse your memory, but I suppose I must remember Angelica, too.'

'You're a hard man, Chico. She still around?'

The dark eyes slitted. 'She works for me when she feel like it.' He bared big teeth. 'She have a – frien' now she like even more than you, Clay. He come from Magdalena, a *ranchero*. That make you jealous?'

Silent shook his head, knowing the man was deliberately provoking him. 'I need her help – or yours.'

Chico's steely smile widened. 'I can not speak for my sister, but it is my pleasure to – refuse you, *señor!*'

'Figured you might. Look, I'm sorry about the trouble I stirred up, Chico, but at least Angelica still has a whole face, doesn't she?' It annoyed him to have to remind Chico so bluntly of an obligation that he seemed to have overlooked.

The Mexican nodded slowly. '*Si – Si*, it was all most *inoportuno*. Ah! It was long time ago.' He lifted the bottle, grabbed a second glass and splashed some of the almost colourless liquid into each. 'We drink to new times, eh?'

'Glad to.' Silent tossed down the tequila and winced again as it scalded his throat. 'Trouble awaits me in Bisbee, Chico.'

The man pursed his purple lips, his eyes steady on Silent's face. 'I think this is true. Kelty is still there.'

Silent swore softly. 'Figured I had enough men against me already. Now *Kelty*, of all people!'

Chico pursed his lips. 'Ah! *problema muy grande!*'

'Yeah, Chico, big trouble. Angelica might still be able to help me, though. Think she will?'

Chico toyed with the glass. 'I not joke about her *ranchero*. But I think maybe she will still do anything you wish, Clay. But you ask her yourself.'

Apparently the singer with the frizzy hair had recognized Silent and brought Angelica in from some back room. She was as beautiful as ever – from a distance anyway – but as she slouched closer, her white blouse straining against her bosom, he saw she was a little more used-looking, and breathing a trifle harder than the occasion called for. Her eyes flashed. Her hair was naturally black once again and her red lips parted, showing white teeth.

'Ah, my *solo lobo*, my *héroe*, has returned.' She brushed against him in the old bold way, eyes flashing with mischief, a brow flicking in invitation. He reached out, touched a smooth, brown cheek.

'It was a long time ago, *querida*.'

Her face straightened and she pouted. 'Ah! Why you use endearments when you do not mean them!' She spread her arms. 'I have a beautiful body, men tell me – some women, too. But you, you did not want it!'

He smiled. 'Could hardly have taken up your offer, Angel, with Kelty's gun in my back.' He stared soberly. 'I think I might be about to give him a chance to do the same thing again. Very soon.'

Immediately her face changed, full of concern now, as she took a step closer, grabbed his arm. He winced – she had chosen the arm where the bullet had seared him.

'*Dio mio!* You already have big trouble, I think!'

'Bigger since Chico told me Kelty's still marshal of Bisbee. Angel, I have to go to Bisbee and see some men.'

Her dark eyes moved over his desert-ravaged face and she saw something there beneath the grit-clogged stubble and the jutting jaw, heard it in his strange voice; this was no ordinary meeting that he wanted. It was very important to him, and, she sensed, also very dangerous.

She glanced at Chico. 'Franco is coming from Magdalena. You could keep him occupied by showing him that river land you wish to sell if I am not here?'

Chico smiled. 'That land which I do *not* wish to sell but which he wishes to buy! But for my sister? Of course. For Señor Clay...' He sobered, then spread his arms. 'Of course, also! We are all amigos here, now.'

The Red Angel squeezed Silent's good arm this time. 'My Franco is jealous, but he is ... manageable. Now, we make plan, eh? So, some *good* tequila, Chico, your best!'

'I'll need some more ammunition, Chico.'

They both gave him a sober look but the bullet-headed Mexican nodded slowly.

'It can be arranged.'

Angelica moved closer to Silent.

'I think this talk will need *two* bottles of Chico's best tequila, *mi solo lobo!* We must make no mistakes.'

Silent agreed with that.

CHAPTER 14

FANGS OF THE WOLF

Marshal Kelty was a pinch-faced man in his early forties. One glance at his eyes and clamped lips told anyone who saw him that here was a man without humour. A man who took his job – and himself – mighty seriously.

Seated at his desk, he looked up from the report he was writing for head office on the indolence of the Mexicans in Naco and its connection with a wave of petty crime, as the Street door opened. He gave a slight start when he saw that it was a Mexican girl who stepped inside out of the blustery night. She shook rain from her straw hat as she removed it and he recognized her at once. Kelty prided himself on such an attribute, boasted he could easily tell one Mexican from another – and remember their names from years earlier.

'Señorita Rojo, the Red Angel herself,' he greeted, not standing, though, and unimpressed by the brief white flash of her smile.

'Ah! You have the good memory, eh?' Angel knew, like everyone else about his boast and she also knew he was susceptible to flattery. A bitter, lonely man, *something* had to give him a little pleasure.

'I can tell you Mexes apart, not like a lot of *Americanos*. What d'you want? I'm due my supper in ten minutes.'

'Then I will not delay you, *señor*. You remember ... but of course you will! So I will tell you without delay–'

'That would be nice!'

'The man who – who thought he was saving me from your deputy, the one with the spurs...' She touched her cheek.

Kelty was straight as a ramrod in his chair now, mean eyes narrowed. 'Aaron Clay? The one I put in Yuma?'

She nodded. 'He is in Naco. He is drinking hard. He make trouble for Chico. My brother try to calm him down but this Clay ... knock him out, smash bottles...'

Kelty was moving to the wall rack now, reaching for his hat with one hand, his gun belt with the other. 'Keep talkin'! I like what I hear! I'm expectin' a posse from Tombstone who're after him but I don't aim to wait.'

'He say he will burn Chico's cantina. The blaze will bring you and he will kill you from the cover of the smoke! He – he *very* drunk and I slip out with my frien', Franco, who insist one of his *vaqueros* ride with me for protection when I come to warn you.'

'Franco? Oh, yeah, that rich greaser from Magdalena, likes to throw his weight around. Clay still there at the cantina?'

'When I left, *sí*. The rain slow us down but Chico tell me I must tell you *pronto*.'

'You did right.' Kelty had his gun belt on now, checked the rifle, making for the door. He paused, looking out of the window, seeing the hunched *vaquero* outside in the colourful poncho, apparently half-asleep in the saddle. He snorted. 'So much for your *vaquero* bodyguard!' he said contemptuously, slipping on a worn slicker. 'All right. You can come back with me or stay. You make up your mind, while I go round up some of my deputies.'

He hurried out into the rain-swept night, glanced briefly once more at the slumped Mexican on the black horse, and strode along the wet boardwalk, making for the closest saloon.

Angelica put on her hat and stepped outside. 'Wait until he goes,' she said quietly and the poncho-clad rider lifted a finger briefly in acknowledgement.

It was barely fifteen minutes before Kelty led his small posse of five men out of town on the southern trail to Naco. It was raining more heavily than ever and it would be a slow ride down, for the trails were twisting and muddy.

The Mexican swung down and stepped under the awning outside the law office. He swept off the large straw sombrero, revealing his stubble of several days.

'Wondered if Kelty was gonna look me over more closely for a minute back there,' Silent rasped, shrugging off the old sodden poncho. It smelled like a wet goat. He took his own hat, crumpled but dry, from where he had had it thrust inside his shirt, set it on his head. '*Gracias*, Angel. If I can, I'll stop by and say *adios*.'

Impulsively, she stepped against him, her rain-cold lips brushing his stubble. 'I know you will not come, Clay. This is very serious business for you. You should have let Chico send some men to help.'

'I've involved you and Chico enough. Still not sure I haven't made a heap of trouble for you with Kelty. I'm desperate, Angel. I've been after these killers for months and now they're all gathered in the one place.'

'And you are one man! *El solo lobo!*' He could hear the edge of a sob in her voice, saw a glisten in her eyes. 'You take too many risks!'

He took her arm, leaned down and kissed her lightly. *'Buenas suerte,* with your *ranchero!* The very best of luck, Angel.'

Her cheeks were wet with tears now but her voice was surprisingly steady when she said, 'I will marry him within the week! Why don't you come to my wedding?'

He wasn't sure whether she meant it or was taunting him in some way, so he smiled faintly, squeezed her arm and swung away into the rain. She put a hand to her mouth, stepped out from under the awning, ignoring the rain.

'Buena suerte to you, too, Clay!' But she knew her words would not reach him above the sudden roar as the rain increased and thundered on the roofs along the street.

A couple of people running to get under shelter glanced at her, but without interest; even a beautiful Mexican woman standing with the rain running off her, was nothing to get excited about in Bisbee.

Silent hurried along the walks, staying under the awnings where they existed, running across the open spaces, searching. He found the Arizona Union Mercantile warehouse in a large corner lot fronting Cochise and Fargo Streets.

Behind was a small, dirty building with smoke stacks. SMELTERY was painted on a peeling sign on one wall. It was too small to be called a 'foundry', but ideal for what Ralls had in mind. Not only could the gold be melted down here, it was within a frog's leap of the border and the yellow metal was a currency that was accepted all over *Mañana* Land, without question as to its origins. There were lights inside and he could hear the roar of a bellows-assisted furnace, the dull clatter of metal tongs and sharp hammer-blows which were probably made as the bars were tapped free of the metal moulds.

They must have figured it was safe enough to melt the gold by now and take it across the border ... or his investigations had forced their hands.

He carried his rifle butt-uppermost so as to keep rain out of the bore. Now he stepped under the awning outside the locked front door of the smeltery, eased his Colt in its holster – wet leather tended to grip a handgun because of its bulges and grooves, the leather moulding itself to the shape – and prepared for his entry.

He smelled hot metal and charcoal now. There was a blurred glow through a filthy window beside the door. He tried to count the moving shadows but there was not enough clarity for that. He only hoped he hadn't missed Ralls. Or Bowdrie.

That was the thought that flashed through his mind an instant before he kicked in the heavy door.

It was a strong kick and the old wood splintered, showering slivers into the smoky room. A group of men were gathered around a forge, some stripped to the waist, smeared torsos gleaming with sweat. Two men were in the process of pouring liquid gold from an iron pot suspended between them on a long-handled cradle, their muscles bulging with the weight. Bright gobbets of gold splashed on to the floor, quickly cooled. But it was the men who weren't working who interested Silent.

He saw Ralls, Will Bowdrie, Bodine and two others who he knew were Ralls's men though he didn't know their names.

They made a stunned tableau for a few seconds, frozen by the shock of his violent entry. Then, as their temporarily numbed brains began to work again, recognizing him, they reacted.

They were pros, scattered, making too many targets for Silent to concentrate on. But he had been prepared for that: it was why he had loaded the rifle fully, ten in the tubular magazine and one more in the breech. He figured he would need as many shots as possible. As the men scattered, one drew and fired with blurring speed, catching Silent off guard. He propped, braced the rifle butt into his right hip and began working lever and trigger, moving the barrel in a jerky arc wherever he saw men running. Glass shattered and bullets ricocheted.

One of the workers yelled and grabbed at his shoulder as he released the cradle and molten gold spilled across the floor in a thick, spreading sheet, cooling rapidly. Lead whined off the cauldron. A handful of glowing charcoal leaped into the air. Bullets buzzed and spattered around Silent.

He dived for the floor, sliding on to his side, palming up his six-gun, although the rifle was not yet empty. He held the Winchester in his left hand, thumbed the six-gun's hammer. One of the unnamed outlaws crumpled. The second man, running towards Silent, skidded and tried to fling himself aside. A bullet caught him somewhere in the body and he spun in a full about-face before falling and crawling laboriously in behind the forge where he slumped.

Bodine made for the dark part of the smeltery, shooting behind him without aiming. One of his shots clipped a work-man's leg and it collapsed under him, the man clutching the bloody wound and screaming curses at Bodine.

Silent wasn't still now. That would be fatal, to just lie sprawled in the one spot, even shooting constantly. He rolled to his right, snapped a shot through the rapidly thicken-ing murk of gunsmoke and charcoal fumes, thrust to hands and knees and launched himself backwards. He hit, skidded around on his belly and beaded Will Bowdrie, who was kneeling beside the forge, having trouble reloading his Colt. Will spilled some cart-ridges and half-stood in an effort to snatch at one still falling. Silent shot him twice, emptying his Colt. He had the handgun rammed back into his holster and his rifle in his hands by the time the killer had fallen – across the glowing forge. Bowdrie screamed and kicked, put down a hand to thrust away from the coals, but screamed louder when his hand sank to the wrist in the red-hot, loosely packed charcoal. He was halfway up when Silent ran forward and kicked his quivering legs out from under him. Falling across the forge, Bowdrie died horribly – almost as horribly as young Larry when he was skinned alive.

Eyes stinging, Silent searched for Ralls, saw Bodine disappearing through a partly open small door in the shadowed part of the foundry and sprinted forward. He slammed into the wall beside it. A bullet gouged wood from the frame and some needle-like splinters tore through his shirt, stinging his flesh.

Warily, he slid along the wall, eased forward enough to see with one eye. Ralls was already mounted, spurring his horse out of the dark yard, spray and mud flying under the hoofs. Silent wrenched his head back as something winked – a fugitive shaft of light catching a gun barrel swinging in his direction.

He saw where Bodine was crouched then, down beside this end of the weathered stables, whitewashed clapboards at his back making him a fine target. He let the man shoot, then stepped into the doorway, blazed two swift shots from the rifle. Bodine reared up, staggering, trying to bring up his gun.

Silent walked towards him, not hurrying, levering another shell into the rifle's breech. Bodine swayed, blood trickling from his mouth, eyes hooded. Desperately, he used both hands to lift his Colt now.

Silent pressed the muzzle of the rifle into the hollow of the man's throat and, looking straight into those pain-filled eyes, pulled the trigger.

There were people crowding into the streets by now, some wanting to know where in hell Kelty was when the town was being shot up by a gang of raiders. It didn't seem possible that one man could fire so many shots and leave so many dead men strewn around.

But they hurriedly opened up for Silent as he came running out of the lane beside the smeltery. He sprinted across the street through the mud and lashing rain to where the big black horse Chico had given him to replace the desert-worn roan still stood drooping at the hitchrail.

He stood under the awning, reloading both guns before mounting. He thrust the rifle into the saddle scabbard, turned the black and lifted it into a gallop down the street, in the direction he had last seen Ralls heading.

The rain didn't let up until midnight. It washed out any tracks Ralls might have made.

But it also covered Silent's tracks and that was in his favour, because he knew that, by now, Kelty would have come roaring up from Naco and set his posse after him.

He wasn't worried about the lawmen, least-ways, he didn't dismiss them completely, because Kelty was a strong hater and he would want Silent's scalp after the happen-ings of the night. If he saw any sign of the posse, he would take precautions accord-ingly.

What he had to do now was catch up with Ralls. The man was in a panic, but he knew Ralls was not the kind to come this far along without having some sort of escape plan. He would have had a way down to Mexico worked out for the transfer of the smelted gold. This was probably the way he would go now.

The watery sun gained heat and bright-ness before mid-morning and Silent rode to the top of a hill, the ground slick and slushy, the black struggling. He had to dismount and drag the reluctant horse to the top, breathing hard from his effort. But it was worth it.

Out there a horse was down, either bogged or with a broken leg. It lurched and struggled several times, trying to get up as Silent watched, way out on the mud flats which glistened like glass, rain-pools catching the sunlight.

And there was a man, stretched out in the mud a few feet beyond the downed horse.

Yeah, looked as though the mount had snapped a leg, slipping in the slime and mud, most likely, and Ralls had been thrown, heavily enough to knock him out. Or maybe he had stopped a bullet and it had finally finished him. Or he had simply broken his neck. Silent hoped not; he didn't want Ralls to die that quickly.

The black slid and weaved and whinnied its way back down the slope of the hill. Silent threw his weight back on its rump, allowing it latitude to prop its forelegs on the truly slimy sections. He held the rifle out to one side, leaning to balance it, and placed his weight as centrally as possible so as to allow the horse to stay on a more or less even keel.

At the foot of the slope the black snorted, shook its head, gobs of mud flying as it stomped more from its legs. The animal was wise enough to know it had to shed this extra weight before the mud hardened.

Silent was impatient, but forced himself to wait out the horse's precautions; he was relying on its strength and fleetness so it only made sense to co-operate with the black's natural instincts.

As far as he could he kept an eye on the downed horse, which was still struggling to rise. He could hear its shrill whickerings now and knew it was in pain. The man beyond it hadn't moved.

He rode out in a wide arc, not easy with him being so close to another rise studded with boulders to the south, within rifle shot. He didn't think Ralls would have a man in there but... He almost hauled rein, thinking he saw a movement in the shadow of a boulder on the slopes. But while he watched closely as he let the black move forward at its own pace, he did not see the movement again, or anything that might indicate a bushwhacker changing position.

He cut in towards the downed horse, which was no longer trying to get up but lying still, occasionally whickering miserably. Silent gave most of his attention to the man now. It was Ralls, wearing a brown corduroy jacket that Silent had seen him in at the smeltery. His hat was still on, but askew, covering half his face. He was lying on his right side, his Colt and holster pinned beneath him, left arm outstretched, the hand empty.

But Silent walked the black around at a distance of several yards, rifle cocked and pointing at the prone man. He sat the horse, studying Ralls, waiting. He could put a shot into Ralls and make sure but there was no satisfaction in him yet. He had killed Bodine and the Bowdries, the men who had butchered Larry, but he wanted Ralls, the man who had ordered it all, to die by *his* hand.

At last, he dismounted and walked slowly forward, rifle ready. Then he noticed the mud on Ralls's right side, the one that faced him as he approached. There was a kind of ridge or ripple just discernible, a small, irregular circle. It didn't look natural but at the same time, wasn't altogether out of place in this churned-up mire.

Suddenly Ralls rolled away, the hand under his body yanking on a rope he had buried just below the surface of the mud after his horse had collapsed under him. The noose whipped tight – and just missed catching Silent's boots. It snagged on the heel of one but his reactions were so fast that he jumped out of the loop. He slipped and went down to one knee, rifle muzzle gouging into the mud. Ralls was coming at him like some flying demon, big body launched as if from a catapult, clawed hands reaching.

Silent had time to notice the man's holster was empty. Ralls had lost his gun and so had rigged this trap, setting the noose on the side of his gun arm, rightly assuming that it was the natural side for Silent to approach.

He drove into Silent like a locomotive, working his shoulder point into the man's midriff, boots scrabbling for a hold, thrusting forward, trying to put Silent down where he would no doubt ram his face into the mud and smother him.

Silent went over backwards, Ralls climbing his body like a slithering snake, hands reaching for his throat. Silent whipped up his knees, caught the other in the belly, and thrust him away. Ralls spilled sideways but reared to his knees, swinging a backhand blow. It missed by a whisker. Silent flung a handful of mud into the contorted face. Ralls was insane with rage – this man, this lone drifter had thwarted all his plans, carefully made and detailed plans, that should have worked and made him mighty rich.

But this unstoppable son of a bitch had stalked him and hunted him down like the wolf he had been named after. Everything was lost now! The only satisfaction that remained was to kill the man who had defeated him.

Roaring, Ralls went in swinging, rage driving him to take stupid risks. It didn't pay off. Silent ducked and weaved, drove knuckles up under the man's ribs, bringing him to his toes, halting him as if he had run into a wall.

Ralls began to sag, swung awkwardly. Silent dodged easily, slammed two shattering blows into the man's face, mud and blood mixing as they flew from his jerking head. Ralls stumbled, went down to hands and knees, and Silent lifted a knee under his jaw. Ralls stretched out on his side in the mud. Silent set his feet to keep his balance, sagged a little, blinking blood out of his eyes.

Then he thought, incredibly, that he heard his name called. Distantly but definitely his name. He turned his head and squinted. He *had* seen a movement up on that other rise after all! There was a horse in the shadow of a rock, someone lying prone on the ground and– God! He had a rifle! He was going to die anyway.

Then he heard a noise behind him. He spun wildly and his heart sank. Ralls was half-erect, holding Silent's Winchester, dripping mud. But the lever worked and Ralls grinned with his blood-smeared broken teeth as he raised the weapon.

'You lose, you bastard!'

His words were followed quickly by a shot, but it sounded all wrong, coming from the wrong direction, not loud enough. Ralls jerked, his body punched back by a bullet. As he went, the rifle sagging, he must have pulled the trigger. The breech exploded, half the barrel clogged with mud. It blew Ralls's right hand almost off, but it was doubtful whether he knew it. A bullet had smashed in his face and blown out the back of his head.

Stunned, senses spinning, Silent dropped to the muddy ground, shaded his eyes and watched as the mysterious rider he had seen on the slope galloped towards him on a claybank horse that he recognized.

'Gail...?' he said hoarsely, but she was too far off yet to hear him.

He had put Ralls's horse out of his misery and washed some of the mud off him with canteen water; there would be no shortage of water after the rain. He had kept her away from Ralls's body: she would find it hard enough to live with the fact that she had killed a man, thanks to her expert shooting, without seeing the mangled mess of Ralls's head.

She was tense and tight-faced, fighting down her reaction to having shot Ralls. She told Silent, with some bitterness, that she seemed to be 'getting used to shooting at live targets'. Then she added that she had tried to find him, to warn him that Lyall had ordered his arrest on a flimsy charge. Maybe the court would throw it out, but Silent would have a lot of trouble before that happened.

'I went too far south and got caught in the cloudburst, had to shelter in a cave,' she said, starting to relax a little. She gestured to the hill behind her. 'I saw Ralls's horse go down and was preparing to ride out to help when he started laying out that noose under the mud. I was intrigued. Then I saw you coming, though I didn't recognize you until you were much closer and approaching him.'

She shrugged, hands twisting, trying to keep control. She glanced towards Ralls but Silent had pulled his corpse in against the horse so that she could only see one leg.

'I owe you – again.'

She looked exasperated. 'You "owe" me nothing! For heaven's sake, I – couldn't just let him kill you. I *had* to do something.' Her voice faltered but she was steadier than he had expected.

'And you did it mighty well.'

'You – you'll be a fugitive now, won't you?'

He nodded. 'Neither Kelty nor Lyall will let this rest. And with my background it'll be hard to shake.' He looked into her beautiful though worried face. 'Say, you ever made a wedding gown?'

She blinked, she was so startled at the abrupt change of subject. 'Of course – but – what a question!'

'Well, there's a wedding coming up in Magdalena – in about a week. Reckon you could run up a gown in that time?'

'I – I suppose so, but–'

'Mexican weddings are great. Lots of colour, tons of food, plenty of dancing, fireworks – a real fiesta.' Just *the kind of diversion she needed right now.*

'I've never been to a Mexican wedding.'

'I've already got an invitation. I'll take you – if you'd like.'

She studied his battered, muddy face and smiled slowly. 'I hope you'll get well and truly cleaned up first! I think I might even have to make you a new shirt.'

'It's a deal.'